I0627376

HOME *for the* HOLIDAYS

D. Allen

DN Publishing

–SINCE 2015–

DAVIDNETHBOOKS.COM

Home for the Holidays
Copyright © 2025 by D. Allen
Batavia, NY

www.DavidNethBooks.com

ISBN: 978-1-963602-77-7
First Edition

Subscribe to the author's newsletter for updates and exclusive content:
DavidNethBooks.com/Newsletter

Follow the author at:
www.facebook.com/DavidNethBooks
www.instagram.com/dnpublishing
www.patreon.com/dnpublishing

Also by D. Allen

<u>Montana Beach</u>
Summer Stay

Summer Job

Summer Nights

<u>Small Town Christmas</u>
A Christmas Reunion

A Christmas Charade

A Christmas Spark

A Christmas Song

A Christmas Departure

A Christmas Wedding

A Christmas Escape

A Christmas Renovation

A Christmas Family

<u>Standalones</u>
Snow After Christmas

Thanksgiving Day Parade

At the Core

Home for the Holidays

THURSDAY,
December 18th

 Prologue

"I think you should just be honest with them," Gary said. He had both hands gripped on the steering wheel, keeping the car straight amidst the snow drifts along Route 33.

"I promise, I will tell them when the time is right," Suzanne replied to her husband. "All I'm saying is I want Christmas to feel like Christmas. We don't need anything else getting in the way. It's bad enough that I need a holiday to get them to come to the house anyway."

Gary was quiet. He didn't have any children of his own to miss, so he didn't know what it was like to have adult children who lived far away and rarely visited. And, despite his best efforts to connect with them,

Suzanne's children hadn't really taken to him, even though he and Suzanne had been married for more than ten years.

"Aren't they going to feel hurt that you weren't honest with them from the get-go?" he asked.

"Well, if they'd been around more, then there'd be nothing to hide from them to begin with!" Suzanne spat. She fell silent as she looked out the window. Then, after a few moments of letting Perry Como croon about going home for the holidays through the radio, she added, "That's not fair. They're all busy. And I'm proud of each one of them. It's just…I wish I had them home more." She adjusted the fingers on her gloves as a distraction. "I guess I just miss the way things used to be when it was the four of us, all the time."

Gary glanced at his wife quickly before returning his attention to the road. He reached over and took her hand with one of his and squeezed it. "I know. Getting older means watching the good moments pass by us, just as much as the bad ones. But there's still good in our lives. And I'll always be here to share it with you."

Suzanne squeezed his hand back. "I know, dear. Thank you. Just…promise me you won't say anything to them?"

He took in a deep breath and let it out slowly. He

very much disagreed with his wife's choice, but Linda, Keith, and Marty were *her* kids, not his. When it came to them, even though they were adults, all he could do was voice his opinion and support whatever decision she made.

"You know I hate this, right?"

She was quiet as she looked out the window while they drove into suburbia. "Yes, I know."

"But I'll respect your choice, if that's the one you want to make."

"It is." She shifted in her seat, settling in to the decision that she'd just made final. "I'll tell them later. But for now, I want a happy Christmas."

Gary smiled at her. "Anything for you, dear."

They remained quiet the rest of the ride to the airport. From their small village of Corfu, the Buffalo Niagara International Airport was just a thirty-minute commute down Route 33, which became Genesee Street closer to the airport and was Main Street in Corfu.

Once they arrived at the airport, Gary navigated the car to the Arrivals lane. They both squinted with the sun glare until they got underneath the bridge for the Departures lane, which was directly above them.

There was a myriad of cars and cabs and ride sharing vehicles trying to compete for the limited parking spots along the curb, all trying to avoid the

airport shuttles zooming by in the left lane.

Gary eyed up a spot and angled the car into it to claim it. He knew he'd have to do a lot of maneuvering to get the car aligned with the curb, but at least nobody was going to take his spot.

"There!" Suzanne shouted. "There she is!" Her voice cracked with emotion. Despite the cold, she rolled down her window and called to her daughter, who was hurrying out of the airport with her suitcase behind her. "Linda!"

Chapter 1

"Mom!" I called back once I spotted hers and Gary's gray sedan among the mass of other vehicles.

I rushed down the sidewalk, pulling my suitcase behind me as the cold Western New York weather nipped at my face.

Mom fumbled with the door, finally getting it open and hurried out to greet me.

"Wait until I get the car in park!" Gary called after her, but Mom wasn't listening.

She left the door open and wrapped me in a tight hug that made me finally feel like I was home. The smell of her, the feel of her arms around me—even if she did feel

a little thin herself—all blended together to comfort me in a way that nothing else could.

"Oh, I've missed you!" Mom said once we parted. She put her hands on my cheeks and stared into my eyes. I did the same, taking in all the ways that she'd changed since I'd last seen her. How much she'd aged. Or was that only because I was constantly surrounded by people obsessed with their looks in New York City?

"How long has it been?" Mom asked.

"I flew you out for Easter," I said with a laugh.

"One weekend! And I had to fly out the night of Easter so you could get to work Monday morning. Besides, that was *months* ago!"

I gripped her hand. "Well, I'm here now, Mom. And I'm staying until after New Year's. You have me for two weeks!"

Getting that time off had been a hassle, but seeing the relief and excitement in my mother's face made it all worth it. Besides, I had to admit that it was nice to see her too. The stress of New York was very much left back in the city.

Mom smiled and took a deep breath as she clutched her chest with her free hand. "Oh, that makes my heart happy!"

Gary, who had given up on parking the car properly, stepped up to the curb. He and I eyed each

other, both of us sizing up the other to see what kind of introduction we were comfortable with. I moved for a quick side hug while Gary attempted a full embrace. The result was an awkward bumbling of body parts being smushed uncomfortably together and we quickly parted without making comment on it.

"Come on, dear," Mom said, ushering me to the car. "We're going to take you to lunch so we can catch up. It's been *way* too long!"

As we climbed in the car and closed the doors against the cold winter chill, Gary grabbed my suitcase and popped it in the trunk.

"So, how have you been?" Mom twisted in her seat up front to face me.

"I've been good!" I started, but stopped when a car behind us beeped. Moments later, Gary opened the door and climbed into the driver's seat.

"We have to get going," he said. "That guy behind us is impatient."

"Take us to lunch, Gary," Mom said with a brightness to her voice. "I need to catch up on everything my baby girl's been doing all year!"

It made my heart warm to hear my mother's terms of endearment again. I missed them. I missed her. This was going to be a relaxing two weeks.

The car behind us beeped again, so Gary shifted

the car into Drive and pulled away from the curb. I think we were all happy to put the airport behind us for the time being.

Chapter 2

The restaurant Mom and Gary chose was just down the street from the airport—if the seven-lane road that passed by the airport could be classified as a "street."

Although the restaurant had a heroic name, it was essentially just a diner, which suited the three of us just fine. The whole place was decorated for Christmas. Several Christmas trees were tucked in corners where there weren't any tables. Picture frames were wrapped to look like gifts. Garland hung along the breakfast bar, adorned with red bows. White Christmas lights lined the soffits around the edges of the restaurant. And, to top it all off, Christmas music played softly over the speakers, which could be heard clearly thanks to the thin crowd.

We settled into a booth, Mom and Gary taking one side while I took the other. The waitress was quick, since it was the middle of the day on a Thursday, and we ordered our food along with our drinks. The waitress was a young, cute little thing. Her blonde hair was pulled back in a high ponytail that swung from side-to-side whenever she moved her head, which was often.

After she left, Mom reached across the table for my hands. "Well, don't hold me in suspense anymore! How've you been? I want to know everything about your life!"

I smiled. "I've been good. You pretty much know everything, anyway." I called her all the time. FaceTimed her at least once a week. Since she was retired, Mom was my go-to person to chat with whenever I had a stretch of city streets to walk or whenever I went on the subway—until service cut out.

I knew that Mom loved our phone calls, but I also knew that no phone call or FaceTime could compare to sitting across from someone—I felt the same way.

This was better than Christmas Day.

"I know," Mom said, "but I still want to hear about it. Don't leave anything out."

I shifted in my seat, wracking my brain for what else I could tell her. "Well, um…work's been good. We're working on an advertising campaign with a new client. It's with an imprint book publisher putting out their first few books. They want to stand out and be creative, which means we need to think out of the box, which is always nice."

I worked for one of the largest advertising companies in New York City. I was one of many graphic designers on staff, but I got my fair share of big clients while also juggling the smaller accounts. It was fun. Creative. Most importantly, though, it paid the bills.

"That sounds exciting," Mom said. "Although, I do worry about you living in New York *City*."

I couldn't help but smirk. There was no way I was ever going to convince my mother that, statistically speaking, I was no more in danger in New York than I was back home. "It's not so bad, Mom. Sure, it has its downfalls, but it also has some really good benefits. Like, for instance, my job."

Mom nodded. "I know, I know."

"She wouldn't have this job if she didn't live there, honey," Gary added.

Mom put her hands up in surrender. "Okay! I get it! But you can't stop a mother from worrying."

I couldn't keep the smile off my face. "Mom, I

promise, if something bad happens to me, you'll be the first to know."

"Oh no, not me! You should call nine-one-one first!"

I exchanged a look with Gary. Even though he and I had never really found a way to click, we shared one thing in common: Mom. And we both knew how neurotic she could be.

"Anyway," Mom pressed on after sensing our judgement. "Are you still seeing that boyfriend? What was his name? Barney?"

"Barry, Mom." I pulled my hands away and adjusted the wrapped silverware set so it was perpendicular with the wall. "And no. We broke up." How did my mother manage to pinpoint the *one* thing in my life I hadn't told her? Was it that obvious that I was evading it?

"Oh." Mom's face fell. "Well, that's okay! You'll find someone else!"

"I know, Mom…" I said with a groan. I kept my eyes down so that I wouldn't have to see the look of pity on my mother's face.

"You're so beautiful, and you have a good job, and you're kind and intelligent," Mom went on. "Nobody would believe that you're thirty-nine."

I nodded, my eyes still trained on the surface of the table. "Yep. You've told me that before." Nothing

quite like your mother pointing out your age to signify how *old* you were. Hey, at least I had my looks!

"Although," Mom went on, oblivious to my disengaged attitude to the conversation, "if you're going to want a family, you're going to need to lock down a man sooner than later."

At that, I looked up at her. I opened my mouth to retort, but the waitress came to the table with the food.

"Okay! Here we go!" She cheerfully passed out the plates of food, naming off each one before she set it down. Once everyone had what they had ordered, she held the tray close to her chest and said, "Do we need anything else?"

Gary looked to us, but both Mom and I were busy inspecting our food now that it was in front of us.

"I think we're all set," he told the waitress. "Thank you."

"Enjoy!"

"So, Mom," I started as I plucked a French fry from my plate, "how have *you* been?" Time to turn the tables.

Now it was Mom's turn to avert her eyes. "I've been fine."

Interesting. Another evasive phrase. I didn't for a

minute believe that everything was "fine." Still, I had made a commitment to myself to not be as invasive as my mother, so I decided to fish for information in a different way.

"I was surprised to hear that you're selling the house." That was the whole reason why I had set aside two weeks to come home for Christmas. Mom had said that she and Gary needed help sorting through things, deciding what to keep, what to sell, and what to insist that my brothers take.

As long as I didn't need to see Keith or Marty, I was okay with that. I liked to keep my involvement with them as minimal as possible now that we were adults.

Mom stopped poking her fork at her salad and looked up at me. Soon, tears were welling up in her eyes. She must've realized how she looked because she quickly recovered and tried to blink them away.

"Yes, well, it wasn't an easy decision," she said. "After all, I raised you kids in that house. It's just…" She looked to her husband for support. "It's just too big for us now." She turned back to her food and seemed to find her strength again because she added, "I've given up on the idea of you or either of your brothers moving in and taking over the house after I pass."

"Mom…" I chastised. Now I felt bad for making

her feel bad. "You've got plenty of life left in you. Stop being so morbid."

"From your lips to God's ears." Mom glanced upward toward the ceiling.

Truth be told, I was sad about letting the house go too. Most of my childhood memories were in that house. The birthday parties and holidays. The fights I used to get in with Keith and Marty. The way I used to sneak in late at night when I was a teenager—probably out to see my high school boyfriend, Lyle. The places I used to hide to overhear things I wasn't supposed to be hearing.

Mostly, I remembered the Christmases there. The way the house stood out on the street—really, the whole village—with its Christmas lights and signs in the front yard. Inside, the house always smelled like vanilla, either from Mom's cooking or from the candles she was always burning. It was like a warm hug, wrapping you up in its embrace.

It was home.

I couldn't wait to experience it all one last time.

"Truth be told," Mom went on, "I've been having a hard time with it. I don't want to see the house go, but I feel like it's…" She paused, caught up in her emotion. "It's time to stop—I don't know—living in a fairy tale, I guess." She shook her head. "You and your brothers have made it clear that you have no

interest in moving back to Corfu. I'll just have to live with that."

I could feel myself softening. I wished that I shared in the same dream as my mother, but I didn't. I had a good life in New York—one that I had created for myself. I couldn't just uproot it all to make my mother happy. Corfu was a small town that gave me a happy childhood. But I was an adult now. I needed to focus on my future. I belonged in New York City now.

"Oh, Mom…" I reached across the table for Mom's hand.

Beside Mom, Gary put his arm around her and she leaned into him.

"It's okay, honey," he said. "You lived there for almost thirty years. It's the longest you've lived anywhere. You're bound to have an emotional connection to it. There's no shame in that."

Mom patted Gary's arm and sat up straighter, forcing herself to stop crying. She wiped away the few tears that had already spilled out.

"Thank you for that. I'll be okay. I'm just sad." Mom looked across the table to me. "Having you home for Christmas will help me relive those memories one more time."

Moms really did know how to emotionally sucker-punch you right in the gut.

Chapter 3

Walking back into my childhood home felt like a sense of relaxation that I hadn't felt in years. Of course, things were slightly different, indicating that time had passed since I had been here last, but yet things were exactly the same in all the right ways.

The kitchen counter still had a pile of newspapers—*newspapers!*—and mail on the end that my mother had always put there in an attempt to clean up, only for it to never move from that spot. Two glasses sat on the counter by the sink, daily drinking glasses that would be washed by the end of the night. A dish towel hung from the handle of the oven—different than the ones I

remembered from when I was younger, but still there.

The warmth of the house, the creak of the floors, and the smell of vanilla all worked together to remove any of the travel stress that I had had all day. Even though I was in such a familiar place, going from bustling Manhattan to the tiny village of Corfu was still a bit of a culture shock. My hometown only had about seven hundred people living here. There were probably that many people who lived in my *apartment building* alone.

"Why don't you take Linda's suitcase upstairs, dear?" Mom said to Gary. "Do you know which room was her old room?"

Gary nodded and he stepped through the kitchen with my suitcase. "I remember."

I was going to tell him not to go through the trouble of lugging my suitcase up the stairs by himself—I could certainly handle it on my own—but the mention of my own bedroom snapped my attention away. "My room? You still have my room as…*my* room?"

Mom shrugged. "Well, sure, dear. It's not *quite* the same as it was, but what were we going to use it for? Besides, you needed somewhere to stay whenever you came to visit."

I offered a sad smile. It was nice to be

remembered, even as I dug roots so many miles away, but I couldn't help but feel a little sad that the room Mom had saved for me had sat empty since I had moved out.

Mom filled a tea pot at the sink before setting it on the stove. She hugged herself and shivered. "Oh, this time of year brings a chill right to my bones. A hot cup of tea will warm me up."

I stepped further into the house and looked around, admiring all the things I had forgotten over the years. Things that were now bringing up endless memories. Memories that were all well-documented by Mom's endless supply of pictures from when I was a kid.

Except, something was off.

"Mom…"

"Yes, dear?" Mom looked up from her perch behind the stove.

There was once a time when the kitchen was blocked off by a wall. But when I was in college, Mom had finally saved up enough money to remodel the back half of the house the way she had wanted to since we had first moved in. Now, the wall was open and the kitchen was only separated by a peninsula, allowing anyone in the kitchen to see all the way to the front of the house.

"You barely have any Christmas decorations up."

I looked at the wooden snowman perched against the wall in the dining area. Probably a decoration meant for a porch, but one that Mom decided to put inside.

The Christmas candles were out, as were a few snowflake window-clings on the front window, but otherwise the house was devoid of any holiday cheer. Quite the contrast from what I remembered from when I was a kid.

It was depressing. Were Mom and Gary spending the last few Christmases like this? Alone. No decorations. No joy. No family.

The guilt I had felt earlier came back tenfold.

"That's because I was hoping you would help me with that," Mom said with a smile. "I didn't forget! I was trying to include you!"

"But…I thought I was here to help you pack up the house?" I asked. "You know, declutter after thirty years of living in the same house?" I figured the Christmas decorations would already be out and, in another week, I'd be helping her to pack them up and ship them off to storage.

Mom made a face. "Oof. Honey, why did you need to add the number of years to that? It makes me sound old."

"Mom, you *are* old."

"Yes, well, at lunch you told me not to dwell on that, now, didn't you?"

I smirked. "Point taken. But let's not get off-topic here. You waited until a *week* before Christmas to put up decorations? That's…not like you."

The Mom I knew would've been the *first* to put up Christmas decorations. And she wouldn't start until after Thanksgiving was over. Sometimes, she even had me and my brothers out at six in the morning the day after Thanksgiving putting up the giant lit-up figurines in the yard and stringing the lights over the bushes and along the front porch.

For a while, our household was so reliable that the neighbors began to say that they didn't officially consider it the holiday season until they saw our house lit up with lights.

And now, the house was still dark a week before Christmas. But then, if Mom was going to sell the house, it could possibly be dark from now on. The neighbors would have to adjust.

So would I.

"Honey." Mom came around the counter to stand beside me.

Clearly, the pain from the memories was evident on my face.

She put her arm around me and leaned her head on my shoulder. "I don't mean to bring down the mood, but there's a sense of…hmm…" She paused as she searched for the right word. "A sense

of…sadness, I guess? Yes, a state of sadness that comes after your kids move out and away and you go from being their sole caretaker to being someone that only gets brief updates from phone calls."

"But Mom, I—"

She put up her hand to stop my interruption. "I'm not blaming any of you, and I don't mean to make you feel bad. I just want you to understand that it's not always easy for me to pull out decorations and put them up with the same enthusiasm I had when I watched the three of you put them up with me. It's hard for me to look back at the Christmas angel you made in second grade or the toilet paper roll candlestick you made when you were in kindergarten. I would much rather have some company when putting up the decorations."

My shoulders slumped. "Mom, I didn't realize…"

Mom shook her head. "Don't worry about it. That's not what I meant to do. Like I said, I just wanted you to understand."

"But Mom—"

The staircase creaked as Gary bounded down the stairs. "Okay! Your suitcase is up in your room, and I pulled out some fresh towels for you to use and set them on your bed. I also pulled out an extra blanket, in case you get cold in the night. Oh, and we have some extra pillows if you need them."

I gave him a tight smile. He was always buzzing around in the background. "Thank you. I appreciate it."

"All right!" Mom chirped happily. She returned to the kitchen, where the teapot had started whistling. "Should we scratch the tea and make cocoa instead?"

At the moment, there wasn't anything that Mom could've suggested that I wouldn't say yes to.

Chapter 4

Mom wasted no time forcing me into her busy schedule. I had already enjoyed cocoa with her on the couch, and helped Gary bring up the Christmas decorations from the basement. With traveling all morning and stopping for lunch, by the time we finished hauling everything out of the basement, it was getting dark, so we decided to wait on hanging the decorations until later.

Even though it felt like I didn't even have an hour to relax, I couldn't help but feel like my mother was stalling. As if she *wanted* to take all afternoon to sip cocoa and pull out the decorations. Almost like she didn't want to decorate just yet.

Of course, that feeling that I had from these subtleties were in contrast to the words that she said. She claimed that all she wanted was for me to help her decorate.

And yet we were waiting *another* day to do it.

By the time the sun had set and Gary had moved to the kitchen to begin working on dinner, I decided that I had finally earned a minute to myself to collect my thoughts. I hadn't been alone since I left my apartment back in New York.

"I'm going to run upstairs and get settled in," I announced.

Mom, who stood beside Gary in the kitchen and was about to put her apron on, stopped in her tracks and set the apron down. "Oh, I'll come with you."

"No, Mom, it's okay. I can find my way to my room. I *did* live here for a long time, remember?"

"Oh, I know, I just want to make sure you're comfortable."

"Get her those extra pillows from the closet!" Gary called from his perch at the stove.

Mom waved a finger in his direction and nodded. "That's right! I'll do that!"

"I think I can find the pillows," I murmured.

"Just let an old lady enjoy some time with her daughter."

Still feeling a little guilty for staying away from

home for so long and thus leading to my mother's unhappiness, I didn't object as I followed my mother up the stairs to the second floor for the first time in a long time. I bit back comments about my mother crowding me. As the week went on, things would subside. They had to, right? And if not, then I was going back to New York after New Year's Day. I could deal with the suffocation for that long.

At least, I was going to try.

The runner in the upstairs hallway had changed, as had some of the family pictures that hung on the walls, but otherwise everything looked exactly the same as I'd remembered it from when I was a kid. It was almost eerie, the way I was able to physically step back into my memories.

The space looked almost exactly the same as it had when I had moved out. Each bedroom was cleaned and each bed was made, including my own bed, which had the towels and extra blankets on it that Gary had left.

"Mom, is anyone else coming?"

Mom had stopped at the closet just at the top of the stairs and was bending over to rifle through the pillows that were haphazardly tossed at the bottom of the closet. She looked around her legs as she bent over. "Huh?"

"Is anyone else coming?" I locked eyes with her,

trying not to think about the fact that I was essentially looking at my mother's rear-end in order to have a conversation with her.

"Why would you think that, dear?" Mom turned back into the closet until she found what she was looking for, then used the doorknob to straighten up.

"It's just that, every bed is made and every bedroom is cleaned." I looked into the room across the hall from mine, which used to be Keith's. Some of his soccer trophies were still perched on his dresser. Things that he didn't want to take when he had moved out.

The saddest part was, there was no sign of dust on his trophies, which meant that Mom had been actively cleaning his room—as well as the rest of ours, presumably. How many times had she been overwhelmed with sadness after the memories? How many times did she want to call us but decided not to? How many times did she pull out the photo albums and look through all the old pictures she had taken of us when were kids?

"What? You think I only clean the house when I have company?" Mom stepped by me into my old bedroom and set the extra pillow on the bed beside the towels and blanket. "Don't forget who *taught* you how to be tidy."

"Okay, then how come you lied to me about

needing help going through things?" I knew this was bordering on confrontational, seeing as I was calling her out for lying, but I needed some level of transparency that I hadn't been getting. Something was up, and I wasn't going to spend the next two weeks trying to figure out what that was.

"Who said anything about lying?"

"Mom, come on! Each room is perfectly put together! On the phone, you made it seem like our bedrooms were complete disasters and that you and Gary needed me to help haul things to a dumpster."

Mom looked away, gesturing around the room. "Well, this is hardly *clean*. Don't even look in the closet, and you have totes under your bed, and I can't *remember* the last time I vacuumed!"

I put my hands on my hips and gave her a hard look. We both knew there wasn't a speck of dirt or dust on the rug. The fresh vacuum lines proved it.

With a heavy sigh, the ruse was over. "Okay fine! I *lied*, if you want to put it so harshly. It's just, you haven't been home in years and I just wanted you to be here for Christmas!"

"Then you should've just *told* me that instead of *lying* to me about it!"

Mom waved her hand as tears welled up in her eyes. "Oh, I've been hinting that I wanted you home for the holidays every year, but you always have

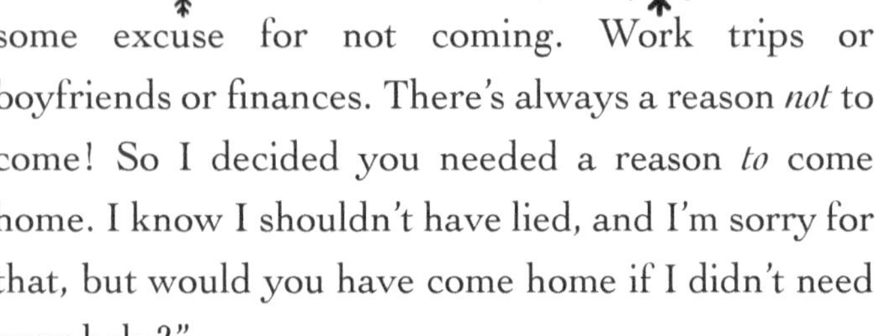

some excuse for not coming. Work trips or boyfriends or finances. There's always a reason *not* to come! So I decided you needed a reason *to* come home. I know I shouldn't have lied, and I'm sorry for that, but would you have come home if I didn't need your help?"

I shifted my feet, then crossed my arms and looked down at the floor. Mom had a point and she had called me out for it. "Ye—yes, I would've come."

"*Now* who's lying?" Mom sighed again. "I wish I didn't have to play tricks on you to get you home. I miss you."

"You've always seemed content to come out to the city and visit."

Mom scoffed. "That's not the same. Don't get me wrong, dear, I love seeing you in your environment. I love seeing how your life has turned out. I just wish I was still a bigger part of that life. I wish I wasn't just a routine phone call."

"You're not just a routine phone call—"

She put up her hand. "I don't want to debate it. I know I'm being selfish. I know what I did was wrong. But when it comes to my family at Christmas, I believe I'm entitled to be selfish every once in a while."

I studied my mother. Any guilt I had felt before was now compounded. When this trip was over, I

absolutely needed to do a better job at keeping Mom in my life. If that meant more trips home, then so be it.

But something about what Mom had said stuck in my ear.

"Wait a minute, you said when it comes to your *family* at Christmas… Mom, are Keith and Marty coming? Because you know the three of us don't get along and I don't want to bicker throughout the holidays and—"

Mom shook her head and took one final step until she was right in front of me. She raised her hands and put them on my cheeks. "It's just you and me, dear. Well, and Gary."

I couldn't help but smirk at that. Gary was *technically* my step-father, but he still didn't always feel like a part of the family. He was always an afterthought, no matter how nice and accommodating he was.

But I could only feel guilty about one person at a time. Otherwise, I might explode.

"I'm sorry, Mom. I don't mean to make you feel…"

"Don't worry another moment about it, dear," Mom said. "It's Christmas. We're together to celebrate." She crossed the room to the door. "I'll let you get settled in by yourself. I know I've been

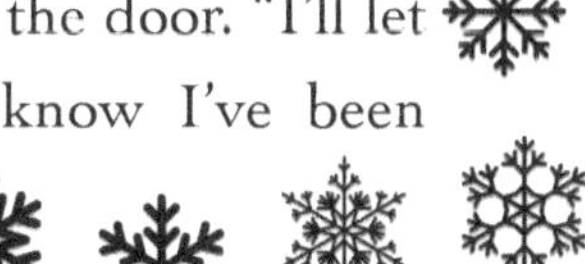

hovering. Gary will have dinner ready soon. We'll call you down when it's time."

She disappeared out the door. Left alone for the first time since I'd been home, I sunk down onto my bed and looked around at my childhood bedroom. I was thirty-nine and yet somehow, I felt the same way I had when I was a teenager.

Funny how coming home worked like that.

Chapter 5

Mom had run out of options. I had laid down my last phase, leaving her with one last chance to lay down her current phase. She was supposed to be putting together a run of nine cards and by the way she kept looking back and forth between the discard pile and her hand, I knew that she was coming up empty.

I sat across the table and leaned on my elbows, a diabolical smirk on my face. "What's the matter, Mom?"

"Just considering my options," Mom replied. She kept her poker face and tried not to admit defeat. She shuffled through her cards again, hoping that a five would miraculously appear.

"Regardless of what you do—or *don't*—lay down, I've won. I completed all ten phases and you're still on Phase Six."

Mom yawned wide, then pooled her cards together and tossed them on the discard pile. "Oh, you're right. I don't have anything." She let out yet another yawn.

I collected the cards and shuffled them a few times before fitting them back into the box. I forgot how much I loved playing cards with Mom. Phase 10 had been a staple when I was younger, back when every holiday was a celebration with extended family. It had always led to laughter and reminisces about good times from the past. Now that my grandparents had passed and all the "kids" were grown up, the holidays weren't nearly as chaotic—even though Mom and I had exchanged our own fair share of stories throughout the game.

Mom yawned again, which prompted me to yawn too.

"Okay." I glanced at the clock. Just after ten. When had I decided to break my promise to myself to go to bed early tonight? "I'm going to turn in. It's late, and if we're going to hit the ground running tomorrow with all this decorating, then we should get started early, which means I need to get to sleep."

Mom nodded as she collected the glasses from the

dining room table. "That sounds like a plan, dear. I'm going to head up to bed myself, just as soon as I've put these dishes in the dishwasher."

I stood and gave my mother a hug. "Thanks for insisting that I come home for Christmas—even if you had to lie about it. I'm glad I came."

"I'm really happy to have you here, dear. Now, get to sleep. We have a big day tomorrow."

Glancing over to the large window in the living room, I couldn't help but feel sad that it was a week before Christmas and no lights had been hung yet. We'd fix that problem tomorrow. "That's for sure. This house seems dark and bare without all the decorations."

Mom nodded. "Tomorrow, for sure."

"Good night!" I called as I stepped through the living room toward the stairs.

My loud declaration rose Gary from where he had fallen asleep on the couch. He sat up and looked around, a little confused.

"Good night, Gary," I said. "See you in the morning."

"'Night," he murmured as he rubbed his eyes.

I disappeared upstairs and dug out my toothbrush from my bag. As I was crossing the hall to the bathroom, I heard Mom and Gary talking downstairs. Whispering, was more like it. And, just

like I did when I was a kid and wanted to eavesdrop, I disappeared into the bathroom, shut the door, and opened the heating vent so I could hear what they were talking about.

It was faint—they really *were* talking quietly—but I could hear bits and pieces of their conversation in the kitchen.

"Shh!" Mom said loudly. "Yes, it's…"

Gary mumbled something, then I heard Mom's voice again.

"I know my kids… …Christmas… …take a little bit of time…"

Nothing too juicy, although I had no idea what Mom was talking about.

I straightened and looked at myself in the mirror. There were dark circles under my eyes. Definitely long past bedtime. I only hoped that I'd be able to get a good night's sleep in my old bed. I wondered if Mom had changed the mattress since I had moved out. Then again, what reason would she have to do that?

I opened the medicine cabinet to look for the toothpaste, but stopped when I saw what else was in there.

Pills.

Lots and lots of prescription pills. Most of them made out to my mother. What did she need all of them for?

I pulled one bottle off the shelf and tried to read the label, but a knock at the door startled me.

"You almost done in there?" Gary asked on the other side.

"Yep!" I called, louder than I had intended. "Just brushing my teeth and then I'll be out!"

I put the bottle back, squeezed some toothpaste on my brush, and tried not to think about what could be ailing Mom that she needed so many prescriptions.

Naturally, only the worst ran through my mind.

FRIDAY,
December 19th

Chapter 6

I felt my stomach drop when I came down the stairs in the morning and saw only Gary sitting at the dining room table. He looked up from the newspaper spread out on the table in front of him, having just taken a sip of his coffee, and smiled at me.

"Good morning." With his mug, he gestured to the kitchen. "There's a fresh pot, if you'd like some. Creamer's in the fridge, sugar is in the cabinet above the coffee pot."

"Thanks." I padded into the kitchen and fixed myself a cup.

Like yesterday when my mother had buttered me up with cocoa, the mugs in the cupboard were the same as

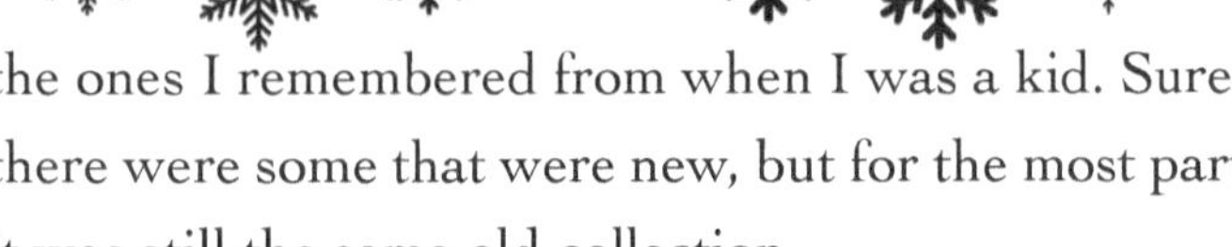

the ones I remembered from when I was a kid. Sure, there were some that were new, but for the most part it was still the same old collection.

There was the dark green one from Lake George that we had gotten one family vacation to the Adirondacks. There was the one from my first marketing job that I had given to Mom to announce the new job. And there were the ones with chips and dings in them, but not so badly that they couldn't be used anymore.

It was odd, how all of those things, seemingly insignificant, helped make me feel more relaxed. More at home. Safe.

"If you're looking for a clean cup, there should be some in the dishwasher," Gary said, pulling me out of my head. "I was going to unload it just as soon as I finish this cup…or the next one."

I smiled at him. "Thanks. I found one." I went with the one from Lake George and filled it from the pot. I used the cream and sugar to doctor it up and then, with no other option, sat at the dining room table with Gary.

The two of us sat in polite silence. Gary still read the paper. I absently looked at my phone, even though I had checked all that I needed to check just before I had gotten out of bed.

It was seven-oh-eight in the morning. This was

sleeping in for someone who was used to getting up at five in the morning every day.

Bored, I locked my phone and pushed it aside, trying not to feel pressure from sitting in silence with Gary. It wasn't that we had a bad relationship. We just…didn't have much of one. Mom and Gary had been married for a little more than ten years, well into my adult life. Other than family functions and other get-togethers — in which there were other people present as buffers — I had never had any one-on-one time with Gary. Whenever Mom would come to visit me in New York, she flew out by herself.

"This is awkward," he said suddenly.

His honesty caused uncontrollable giggles to burst out of me. "Yeah, it is. Sorry."

"It's not your fault. Just the way things are. What do you say we change that?"

"How?"

He shrugged. "By talking, I guess? Find a way to no longer be strangers who just happen to be related."

I smiled and wrapped my fingers around the warm mug. "I'd like that."

We fell into another silence, then Gary leaned over and said, "You start."

I couldn't help but giggle again. Why hadn't I ever realized that Gary had a good sense of humor?

"Um…" I looked down into my cup, hoping that a good conversation starter would be in there. Something that would relieve the tension and make talking a little less forced. "I don't know."

"How about we start with an easy one," he suggested. "How did you sleep?"

"Good," I said quickly, grateful that we had at least *something* to talk about. Even if it was superficial. "Although," I added for more depth, "it did feel a little weird to be back in my childhood bedroom after all these years—especially since it looks almost identical to how I left it. Kind of like time traveling."

"It's not quite like time traveling." Gary sipped his coffee and smirked at me over the brim. "Trust me, I've done it."

I rolled my eyes with a smile. He certainly had the dad jokes down.

"And as for the museum to your childhood, you can thank your mother for that one," he added. "Anytime I suggest making any kind of changes to any of the bedrooms you kids left, she always has some sort of rationalization. What if you need to move back home, what if Keith and his family come to stay—then they'd need *two* rooms!" He shook his head with a smile. "The best I could do was persuade her to upgrade Marty's bed to a queen, but that was

only because that bed was *shot*. Your brother did a number on that one."

"Considering the age he was when he stopped wetting the bed, I would say so…" That comment was spiteful, but it was just like Marty to make a mess and then leave it for *Mom* to take care of. As if he wasn't a thirty-year-old man who should've been able to take care of himself on his own.

"To be fair, she had removed the mattress just as soon as your brother grew out of that," Gary said. "As long as I've lived here, that room has been pee-free."

I cringed. "Okay. This conversation is territory that's too gross to get into before I've finished my first cup of coffee."

He held up a finger in her direction. "But it was a conversation."

"True." Although, Marty was not someone I cared to discuss more than I had to. It wasn't that I was embarrassed by him. He was just an eternal man-child. Completely immature, despite his age, and never took accountability for anything. And I wasn't going to coddle him anymore, even if everyone around him always did.

Growing up, it was Mom, or me, and sometimes even Keith who would have to clean up Marty's messes. The time he stole seatbelt buckles from the

school bus, *I* had been the one to find them and turn them in to our mother. Or when I found the fart bombs in his backpack that he had intended to set off at school. Or when Mom was left in tears when he decided to live with our cheating father full-time instead of seeing him only on special occasions like me and Keith had done, it was *me* who had consoled Mom—at least until she found Gary.

Now that I had a choice, I was selective about who I let into my life. My father, who seemed disinterested in a relationship with us, was the first to be cut. And now my brothers, especially Marty, were also cut from my life. Too much history. Too much drama. Too much stress that I didn't need in my life anymore.

"I believe it's your turn to pick the next topic of conversation," Gary cut in to my thoughts. "Unless you've grown tired of our exercise already."

"No!" I blurted. Now that I had taken inventory of all the people—all the *family*—I had cut out of my life, I was determined to make amends with the one person who was actively trying to connect with me. "No, I haven't grown tired of it. I just…" I sighed and looked down at my cup again. "I guess I just want to know how things are going around here. Really."

Gary's demeanor seemed to change. His casual jokes and easy banter were gone as he debated

something with himself. "The truth is—"

"Good morning!" Mom cheered as she came down the stairs. She was dressed for the day in her holiday sweater already. I wondered how much she had been listening in to our conversation at the top of the stairs. Not that there was much to listen in on.

"My, you two are up early!" Mom greeted Gary with a kiss, then came around to kiss the top of my head before making her way to the kitchen to pour herself some coffee.

"It's after seven, Mom," I said. "It's not that early. You're usually up by now."

Mom came to the dining room table with her mug in hand. "Well, I guess I was tired last night."

"You've been having a lot of days like that," Gary added.

I studied him. Was that his way of answering my question without coming out and saying it? I wondered what he was hiding—and what he had been about to tell me.

"Oh, don't worry about me," Mom said. "It's a good thing I got that extra sleep because we have a big day today. Come on, you two! Up and at 'em! We're decorating for Christmas today! Let me put on some music."

As she disappeared into the living room and knelt down by the shelves with the Christmas CDs, I

looked over at Gary and tried to read his expression. He was stony now as he watched his wife, making it hard for me to tell exactly what he was hiding.

I knew one thing for certain, though: he *was* hiding something. And I was willing to bet my mother was too.

Chapter 7

It was his fault they were leaving so late.

Keith had heard it over and over again as they did the final packing. Wendy had reminded him when he loaded up the car. It had come out when they hit a snow squall on Transit Road in Orchard Park. Then again as the sun began to set, quickly casting everything into darkness and requiring Keith to rely on his headlights to navigate the road, which was made especially worse as more snow began to softly fall.

All the while, Keith had held his tongue. Wendy was upset with him, but it had nothing to do with the reasons she said. They had only been married for about three years now, but it was still long enough for him to know what was truly bothering her.

Wendy flopped back in her seat after twisting around to check on their one-year-old son, Connor, in the backseat. "Great," she spat. "He's asleep. Which means he'll have a hell of a time getting to sleep tonight. Happy?"

Keith shrugged. "Then I guess I'll fight with him to get him to sleep tonight."

She crossed her arms and looked out the window. The mood in the car was in stark contrast to Mariah Carey on the radio cheering about all she wanted for Christmas. Keith considered turning it off, but decided against it. They needed the buffer if they were going to keep falling into tense silences. Plus, it couldn't hurt to have something cheerful on the radio while they bickered.

"No, I'll put him to sleep tonight," Wendy finally said in a softer tone.

Keith knew how much she felt guilty whenever she needed to offload parenting responsibilities — even onto her own husband. The fact that she simultaneously complained about those same responsibilities didn't seem to come into consideration for her.

"Your mom has a separate room for him, right?" she asked.

"That's what she said, yes." He bit back the part

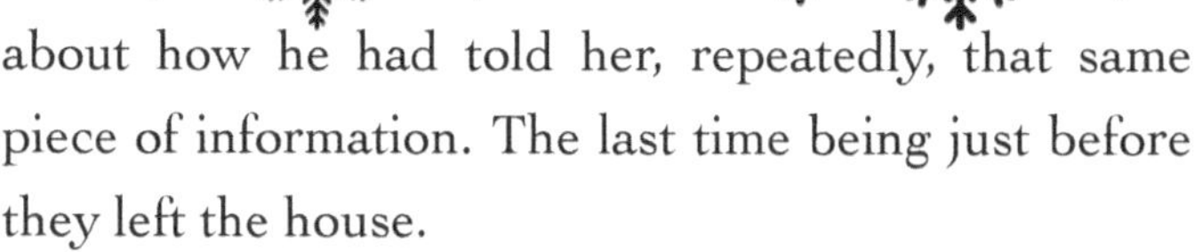

about how he had told her, repeatedly, that same piece of information. The last time being just before they left the house.

"Watch the road!" Wendy braced herself against the dashboard, as if she was expecting the car to strike something hard.

Keith, meanwhile, had seen the light change from green to yellow with plenty of time to slow down and stop before it turned red. "I've got it, honey." 

"You drive too fast," she snapped after the car  had stopped moving. "The roads are slick."

He bit his tongue. 

"Does your mother even have things to do while  we're there?" she asked.

"Christmas things, I'm sure," he responded.  "She's going to want to see Connor. Catch up with us. I'm sure we'll probably play cards or something like  that to pass the time. Why?"

"Well, I was thinking that if we were bored by the  end of the week, we could head home and—"

"No." He shook his head, not allowing her to  even finish her thought. "Absolutely not. We're spending the week with my mother—and Gary—for  Christmas. We're not leaving because we're *bored*."

"What about Connor?" 

"What *about* him? He's one. He laughs when you  blow in his face. He'll be fine."

She scoffed and sank back in her seat. "I don't understand why we need to spend the *full week* with your mother anyway. We're not even going to see my parents for Christmas! How do you think they'll feel?"

"They understand, which is exactly what they told us when we said we were going to go to my mother's this year." He looked over at his wife, who seemed determined to be in a bad mood. She loved his mother, and welcomed her to every family function. Her annoyance at the moment was from something else. Something he understood but didn't have an immediate solution to. "We also have dinner with your parents at least once a week. They'll be fine. My mother, on the other hand, hasn't seen Connor since his birthday party a month ago! I'm sure that's eating her up."

Wendy let out a heavy sigh, but didn't offer anything else. Keith knew that was her way of admitting defeat.

They passed by more cornfields that had been long since plowed, and were now covered in snow, which the wind used as ammunition to carry snow drifts onto the road. Keith navigated the car safely through the drifts, having been driving in winter weather his whole life. Soon, they arrived in Corfu and came to stop at the one light in town.

Keith reached over and put his hand on his wife's knee. It was a silent form of comfort. A way to tell her that he understood just what exactly she was nervous about and that he was there for her. A whole conversation exchanged with just one simple gesture.

Wendy reached down and gripped his hand with hers. She understood too. This week was going to be hard, but not for any of the reasons she had just doled out. And not in any way that people would be able to easily see for themselves.

Chapter 8

It was finally starting to feel like Christmas. We had spent the whole morning decorating the house, playing Christmas music and dancing along with laughter. I had lost count of how many cups of tea and cocoa Mom had made for me. The only thing that could make it feel *more* like Christmas was for an argument to break out between me and my brothers, which always happened when we were growing up. Luckily, neither Keith nor Marty would be spending the holidays with us this year.

By the afternoon, after a morning of dancing and decorating, Mom had noticeably slowed and, after taking a break from decorating to eat the lunch that Gary had prepared—turkey sandwiches and a shared bag of chips between the three of us—Mom had gone upstairs to take a nap. Gary wasn't much further behind as he settled in on the couch, which left me time to catch up on some work emails and read my book.

I had never known Mom to take a nap in the middle of the day before, but then she wasn't as young as she once was. If she needed a rest in the middle of the day, then she should take one. There were certainly days when I could use one myself.

With Gary on the couch, I took the recliner and replied to some work emails on my laptop before setting it aside and pulling out my book. I was five chapters in when I noticed how much the sun had shifted. While the light had been making its way across the carpet as the sun moved in the sky outside, there was currently no direct sunlight coming from the windows.

I glanced at the time and saw that Mom and Gary's naps had lasted nearly two hours.

I put the footrest of the recliner down, which stirred Gary's slumber. I got up and poured myself a glass of water and tried not to think about the medicine cabinet filled with pills upstairs. I couldn't remember whether Mom had had that much medication the last time she came to New York to see

me. Surely, if she had, I would've heard the rattle of them in her luggage, right?

"Does she always take naps?" I asked Gary after he had joined me in the kitchen for his own drink.

"Who?"

"Mom."

He glanced toward the staircase as he considered her question. "Yeah, I suppose so."

"Hmm."

"What is it?"

I shook my head. I was overreacting. Acting just like mother. I needed to let it go. "Nothing. It's just…she never used to take them."

He sighed heavily and then pulled out a chair at the dining room table and slumped down into it. He gestured to the chair across from him and I took a seat.

"Your mother—"

"Oh, wow!" Mom said as she came down the stairs. "I didn't think I would sleep so late! Oh my, we need to get going if we're going to finish putting up the tree tonight."

Gary looked a little disappointed. Still, he turned to his wife and then looked toward the living room. "Everything's all ready to go. I can help put the tree together, then if you girls wanted to finish up, I can make dinner again tonight."

Mom looked at her watch. "Oh wow, is it almost that time already?"

"Not quite." I held my stomach, still feeling full from lunch. The chips had been a treat. Rarely did I ever eat such junk food, but I had been craving it lately. I had been craving a lot of junk food lately. Then again, the Christmas season tended to do that to you.

Putting up the tree was simultaneously the best and worst thing to put up at Christmas.

As promised, Gary did the bulk of the work putting the tree together—we'd had the same fake tree for years. He had barely secured the final piece together before Mom stepped forward and began fluffing out the branches that had been squished down while in storage.

I soon joined my mother—even though I *hated* this part of the process. Glancing outside again, I noted that the sun had almost set. The shortest day of the year was in two days and yet somehow, I still hadn't adjusted to the idea of a four-thirty sunset, especially when Mom had just woken up from a nap about an hour and a half ago.

"Mom, I think that's good." I stepped over and looked at the Christmas lights, but Mom was still fussing with the tree.

"Just…a few…more…" she murmured to no one

in particular as she continued to fluff branches, including spots where I had already gone through.

"Honey," Gary said gently, "I think that's good enough. Nobody is going to notice the spot in the back by the window. All they're going to see from the street is the glow of the lights."

"Yeah," I added. "Besides, after we put the lights and the garland and the ornaments on, the way the branches look won't matter as much."

"I'll notice." Mom stood back and studied the tree.

Gary and I exchanged glances, which brought a smile to my face. This was the version of my mother that I was used to seeing, and it was nice to see that after all these years she was, at heart, the same woman I had loved my whole life.

"There." Mom made one final adjustment then took a step back and inspected our work — *her* work. "I think that'll do it."

"Then let's do the lights," Gary said quickly. He brought the spool over and handed me the end to plug it in and test the lights before we put them on the tree.

No matter how old I was, the glow from the lights always brought a sense of magic and wonder to my eyes that made my soul warm up at the sight of them.

Gary and I worked together to string the lights

around the tree. Meanwhile, Mom followed behind, fixing everything that we had just put on the tree. If anyone was watching through the window, especially as darkness quickly arrived, it must've been a funny sight to watch three grown adults circle around the Christmas tree over and over again.

After the lights were strung, we repeated the same silly routine for the garland. That left only the ornaments to put up.

Mom hauled the large tote of ornaments onto the couch so they could see them better. When she slumped them onto the seat of the couch, she leaned on the back of it to catch her breath.

"Mom, do you need help with those?"

She swatted away my hand. "I can get it! I'm not dead yet." She opened the tote and carefully pulled out an ornament and studied it. "Oh wow. So pretty."

"Yeah." I reached in the tote and pulled out one I had made in second grade. A cardboard circle with pinecone pieces glued on it and a pipe-cleaner bow added at the bottom. I loved pulling out old ornaments. It was a walk down memory lane, which had been par for the course with this trip so far.

Mom and I put up a few ornaments on the tree before I noticed something out the window. Headlights pulled in the driveway. I watched, expecting the car to back out and head back in the

direction it had come from, but instead it stopped behind my own car and the lights turned off. As the interior lights came on, I saw who it was and was immediately filled with rage.

I spun around to face my mother. "You invited Keith!?"

Mom wasn't bothered by my outburst and came to look out the window herself. "Oh, he's here!"

"So you *knew* he was coming, then?" I was fuming. So much for my quiet, relaxing week at home with Mom.

Noticing the tension, Gary quietly disappeared from the room.

Mom ignored me and turned to him. "Honey, go see if they need help with their bags. I'm sure they have a lot of stuff to bring in for Connor."

"Mom, answer me."

Finally, she turned back to me. "Oh, sweetie, lighten up. It's Christmas!"

Without waiting for a reply, she followed Gary out to the side door to greet the new arrivals.

Meanwhile, I stewed beside the Christmas tree. Actually, I pouted. It was childish; I was fully aware of that, but I couldn't help it. The warm, fuzzy memories I had been feeling moments before had now turned sour. Instead, I was reminded of every argument and fistfight and prank me and my

brothers used to play on each other.

But as I watched through the window while Mom and Gary greeted Keith and Wendy with hugs, I couldn't help but feel like an outsider. *I* had removed myself from this reunion. Frankly, I was being petty. We were adults, not kids anymore. It was time for us to grow up. I was the oldest, after all. I needed to set the example.

What finally convinced me was the sight of Wendy pulling a sleepy Connor from his car seat. It killed me that I had never met my nephew before. And I was never going to have a relationship with him if I continued this war with my brother.

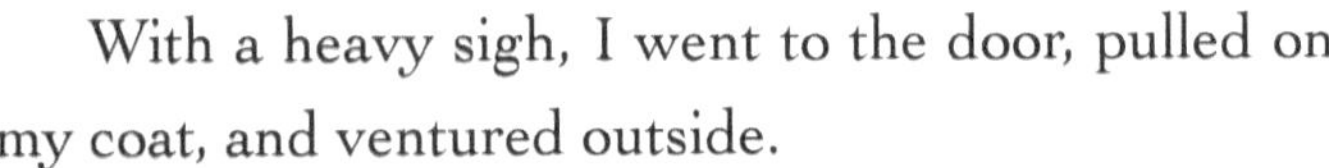

With a heavy sigh, I went to the door, pulled on my coat, and ventured outside.

Chapter 9

Keith hugged Mom tight, even as the wind blew snow in his face. I could tell by the way he closed his eyes and fully wrapped her in his arms that he missed her. As I stood on the porch and watched the exchange, I couldn't help but wonder how often Mom saw him and Wendy.

Nobody said anything as mother and son embraced, even though Mom held on to him for a lot longer than what was normally socially acceptable. She had done the same for me when she had picked me up at the airport yesterday.

When Mom finally did let him go, she reached up and held his face in her hands. "Oh my goodness, you're so handsome!"

"Mom…" he said with a groan, even as the hint of a smile met his lips.

The smile, however, was immediately wiped away when he looked up and saw me. I hugged my body against the cold, kicking myself for not putting anything thicker on to greet him. I offered him a small smile, an olive branch of sorts. Regardless of how I felt, we were going to be spending the holidays together. No sense making it miserable. I could at least be polite.

Keith walked up the few steps and leaned in to me for a quick hug. I opened my arms to receive it and was a little thrown off when he pulled away quickly. Definitely *not* the warm greeting he had given our mother.

Since I was standing right at the edge of the staircase, he took a few steps back down after he gave me the awkward hug. But instead of turning away to handle the logistics of bringing in the bags, he looked at me.

"Linda." He said it in such a polite tone.

"Keith." I matched his energy.

"It's been a while."

"It has."

We studied each other for a while. Neither of us really knowing what else to say to each other. It had been so long since we'd had a conversation. The last

time was at his wedding. I was, admittedly, salty that he was the first of the three of us to get married and I didn't have my best attitude on that night. He was short with me and eventually called me a bitch after my bad attitude got in the way of his happy day.

After that, I didn't care to talk to him for a while and since I lived on the other side of the state, it made it easy to keep our distance. That was three years ago. And now, here we were, about to spend a whole week together after the falling out on his wedding day.

Keith turned and gestured to Mom, who had taken Connor from Wendy. "I had a baby! Well, Wendy did."

At the mention of Connor, I smiled. "I know. Mom sent me pictures. He's beautiful. Congratulations."

"Thanks."

We fell into quiet awkwardness again. Both of us staring at Connor. All of us freezing from the weather. The snow continued to fall and blow in the wind. The light from the porch was only doing so much, given the conditions, and Keith and Wendy still had a lot of things to bring in.

"How about we move this reunion inside?" Gary suggested. "Let's get the baby out of the cold."

"That's a great idea!" Mom tucked Connor closer

to her chest against the cold and hurried up the porch steps.

As Mom passed by, I finally got a clearer view of my nephew in the snowy night. "Baby!? He's hardly a baby anymore! He's so big!"

Keith beamed. "Yeah, he's a tank. He just turned a year old a few months ago."

Mom and I stood and cooed at the baby while Keith and Wendy dug in their car for their belongings.

Gary called from the back of their SUV. "Keith! Does all of this need to come in?"

"Yeah." Keith walked over to help.

"We had to bring half the house with everything we needed for Connor," Wendy explained to Mom and I as she walked up on the porch.

Mom laughed. "Babies don't travel light, that's for sure. Come on, let's get inside and warm up. The guys will bring in the bags, don't you worry about it."

Chapter 10

"What is *this* one?" Wendy laughed as she pulled another handmade ornament out from the storage tub. It was a styrofoam ball with a piece of red felt glued to the top, one googly eye, and a cotton swab hanging on by a thread.

"That's Santa!" I said. "How can you not tell?"

"Who made this?" Wendy turned it around to inspect the name scribbled terribly on the back.

"Oh, that Santa?" Mom asked from the couch, where she was holding Connor in her lap. "That was Keith's. He made it in kindergarten, or first grade. The year should be written on it somewhere."

"It's seen better days," Wendy said.

"What? You don't want to hang Scary Santa on the tree?" I teased. It had always been easy for me to get along with Wendy, despite whatever happened between me and Keith.

"I'll leave that up to my husband."

Keith came down the stairs. "Leave what to me?"

Wendy turned and showed him the ornament. "What do you think? Should we hang this precious gem up on the tree?"

Keith sat on the couch beside Mom and stretched out until his feet were on the coffee table. "I don't care. Do what you want."

Connor began to fuss in Mom's lap.

"He's probably hungry," Keith said. "I can feed him."

"No, let me," Mom insisted. "You help your sister decorate the tree."

"Oh, that's a good idea!" Wendy said. "It'll be like a trip down memory lane—except, I wasn't there, of course. But now I'll get to see it live."

Keith and I exchanged looks before both of us quickly averted our eyes. The message exchanged between us was clear: neither of us wanted to do anything more together on this trip home than was necessary.

"Mom, come on," Keith said. "They're pretty much done with the tree anyway. Besides, I've been

working all day—all week. The kids have been *wild* this week."

Keith was a high school English teacher, which was funny because from what I remembered, he was a terrible student.

"Honey, it's not going to hurt to help out a little bit." Mom stood and handed Wendy the whiny baby.

"Mom, he doesn't have to," I added.

"I think it would be nice for the two of you to reconnect," Wendy said from the chair beside Gary's recliner.

He, notably, sat there quiet. As he usually did.

"I'll just finish the tree myself," I said. Then, under my breath I added, "Not that he ever helped much anyway."

"Excuse me?" Keith sat up straighter on the couch. "I helped!"

Guess I hadn't said it as quiet as I had thought.

"Sure, when it was time to put the star at the top of the tree," I said, "and then *all of a sudden*, you came out of the woodwork and complained that you *never* got to put up the star, even though you weaseled your way into doing it *every year*."

Keith scooted to the edge of the couch. "Maybe I wouldn't have to insist on putting up the star every year if you actually let someone else help for once."

I gestured to Wendy, then over to Mom, who had

gone into the kitchen to get Connor a bottle of milk. "Mom and Wendy have been helping me. What do you call that?"

"Oh, so has New York loosened you up?" Keith asked. "Or are you still fixing what everyone else puts on the tree because you need it to be perfect? Even *Mom* couldn't meet your standards."

"That's not true," I countered. "But is it so bad to want symmetry on the tree?"

"It's more than just symmetry, Lin! Look at it! You're putting up handmade friggin' ornaments and yet it looks like it's right out of a catalog! And you're not even done!"

I shook my head. "Oh, please. You're exaggerating."

Mom returned to the living room armed with a baby bottle and a wooden spoon. "All right!" she hollered over the roar of our argument. "That's enough!"

Wendy took the bottle from Mom's other hand, then shifted in her seat so that Mom wouldn't hit her or Connor with the spoon. She glanced over at Gary, who returned the *what-did-we-marry-into?* look. Connor, meanwhile, was mystified by his grandmother waving a spoon in the air.

Mom pointed the spoon at me, then Keith. "I asked you both here so I could spend Christmas with

my *adult* children, and yet here you are acting like a couple of *brats*. Apologize to each other."

"Mom…" Keith groaned.

"Don't make me use this!" she warned, then waved the spoon in my direction.

"Mom, this is ridiculous," I said.

Mom responded with a swift flick of the spoon against my arm. The pain stung. It was a good thing I was wearing a sweater, otherwise it would've hurt worse.

"Ow! Mom!" I protested as I reached for my arm.

"Ha ha!" Keith mocked.

Mom smacked him just as hard as she hit me. "Apologize, or you can both go home tonight." Then, in a soft voice, she turned to Wendy and Connor. "But not you two. You're more than welcome to stay." She spun around to face us, threatening us with the spoon.

"*She's* the one who brought up something that happened a million years ago," Keith said. "She should apologize first."

"*Me?*" I asked. "What about *you?* You were the one who refused to help!"

"That's because you're already—"

More intense pain in my arm when Mom smacked us both again. Harder this time. "All I

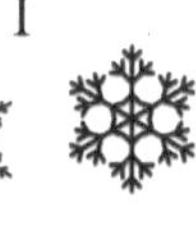

wanted was to relive some of our *good* family memories of Christmas with you kids growing up. I did *not* want to ignite years-old bickering between the two of you. You're both in your thirties—grow up!"

She had a point. We were better than this. It had been a long time since I had acted so petty and I hated how quickly Keith pulled me back down to that level. I let out a heavy sigh, turned my eyes down to the floor, and mumbled, "Sorry."

"Sorry," Keith spat.

"You two better learn how to get along because otherwise I'll be pulling this out a lot more than I should at your age!" Mom turned and stormed off back into the kitchen, throwing the spoon in the sink once she arrived.

Meanwhile, in the wake of everyone's silence following the argument, Burl Ives sang out "Holly Jolly Christmas" over the radio.

Chapter 11

This was the worst.

Not only was I annoyed with Keith for what he had said to me, and for him just *being* here, but now we all sat in uncomfortable silence as we ate the pasta and meatballs that Gary had made. The only sounds were the Christmas music playing softly on the radio from the living room, our silverware clinking on the bowls, and Connor giggling and slamming his fists on the tray from his traveling high-chair.

At least there was a bright side to Keith's arrival. Connor was here too. I loved my nephew. And having Wendy here was nice to have someone other than my mother and Gary to make conversation with. But I could do without my brother, who, at best, made things *uncomfortable*.

Much like this dinner.

Nobody made eye contact with one another. Mom sat at the head of the table and glared in mine and Keith's direction. She only picked at her food. Meanwhile, I tried to avoid her gaze as much as possible and pretend like the food in my bowl was suddenly the most interesting thing I had ever seen, all while trying to pace myself so I wouldn't be the *first* person up from the table, but also not the *last*.

Keith was the first to finish. He stood and began to carry his bowl to the sink, but Mom waved her fork at him and motioned him back down. A mean look was on her face. "Sit!" she commanded.

He obeyed.

After about five seconds of the most intense silence, he finally said, "Mom, this is ridiculous! I'm sorry, okay? I'm sorry for arguing with Linda while putting up the tree. I'm sorry for—"

"You're damn right you're sorry!" Mom snapped.

Everyone stopped and looked at her. This was one of the rare moments where Mom swore. Sure, she had done it a lot when we were kids. We certainly knew how to push her buttons. But since I've been on my own, I think I could count on one hand how many times I'd heard my mother cuss. After tonight,

I'd have to start counting on two hands.

Suddenly, I felt the intensity hit me. Mom was staring daggers right at me. My mind went blank, even as I tried to rack my brain for what I could possibly say to her that would pacify the situation. This morning, I had been her favorite child. The one who had come home to spend Christmas with her. Now, I was suddenly fifteen again, being scolded at the dinner table for bickering with my brother.

"And where is *your* apology, Linda?" Mom left no room for negotiation. An apology would be coming.

"I'm sorry, but Mom, he was just laying around and I was putting up the tree by my —"

Mom put up her hand and I stopped mid-sentence. She looked between the two of us again, ignoring Connor's gleeful cheers and Wendy's quiet politeness as she excused herself from the table to clean him up.

I should've had kids.

"You're both grown adults," Mom said. "You should know better than to talk to each other like that. Than to *act* like that in *my* house! I didn't ask you to spend the holidays with me so I can yell at you. That's something I would fully like to leave in the past."

"Mom, I'm—" Keith started, but one sidelong glance in his direction from Mom shut him up quick.

Finally, she turned back to her food, slowly cutting a meatball in half, then into quarters. "To fully apologize, the two of you will be spending the day with me tomorrow to run errands. I have some last-minute Christmas shopping to do as well."

"The *day*?" Keith groaned.

Mom nodded, keeping her eyes on her food. "Yes, if that's what it takes to finish everything on my list. Just the three of us. That way, the two of you can learn how to behave around one another without acting like children. Understood?"

"Mom, I'm sorry," I said, casting a pleading look in Gary's direction. He sat stoically beside Mom, his napkin clutched in his hands, which were propped up on the table in front of him.

"Yeah, I've been working all week and I was looking forward to relaxing tomorrow," Keith said. "It's not very often we get a lot of time off before Christmas and I want to be able to enjoy the holiday without feeling rushed—"

Mom waved her fork at us to silence us. Even with her mouth full—even though we were adults— she was able to control us without speaking a word. When she finally finished chewing, she said, "No matter how old you are, I'm still your mother. And when has my decision ever been up for debate?"

Keith's shoulders slumped. "Never."

I shook my head in agreement.

"So my decision is final," Mom said. "Now, Keith, if you're looking to relax, I suggest you take the opportunity to do that now. I want to leave by eight o'clock tomorrow morning. Don't make me late because you're too busy *primping* in the bathroom."

I snorted a laugh.

Mom turned on me. "And you should turn in, too, dear. It took us all day to decorate and it really shouldn't have taken that long."

I stared wide-eyed at her remark, but kept it to myself. It only took us so long because of *her*. But arguing that point was going to go nowhere tonight. Instead, I simply nodded, retrieved my bowl from the table and deposited it in the sink before retreating upstairs. Keith and I didn't make eye contact.

It was going to be a long week.

SATURDAY,
December 20th

Chapter 12

I tried to look at the bright sides to my punishment.

For one, I would get to spend another day with Mom, becoming a sort of fly on the wall as I watched the way that she interacted with the world.

For two, I would get to see more of the places where I spent so much time growing up. Not that the trip to the grocery store or the post office had been top on my list to revisit, but regardless it would bring back memories.

And finally, maybe this forced trip would require me and Keith to get over past annoyances and become civil with one another. No doubt that was Mom's plan.

My optimism fell flat when Mom forced both me and Keith to sit in the backseat of the car, like we were both

five years old. Only, we were grown adults so with the two of us in the back seat together, we were practically on top of each other. Definitely not the way I wanted to spend my Christmas break.

"Mom, can I sit up front?" I asked.

Either she couldn't hear us over the roar of the Christmas music from the radio, or she was ignoring me. Either way, she didn't respond as she—very awkwardly—navigated the car out of the driveway and onto the road.

"Guess not," Keith muttered to me.

I turned to the window, figuring that I would just turn inward until my crimes to the family had been paid.

The first stop was the grocery store, but since Corfu didn't have a grocery store anymore, we had to travel to Batavia, a fifteen-minute drive.

The closer we got to town, the more memories came back to me. The familiar houses along Genesee Street—some of them painted new colors, others showing their age. The diner that had changed hands several times since I was a kid. The trees that had been cut down, some new ones planted in their place.

Funny how such simple things transported you back in time.

As Mom traveled up and down the rows of

parking spots at Tops, Keith spoke up from beside me.

"Hey, can we sit in the car?"

"The car?" I asked before she could respond. What was he thinking? It would be freezing if she left us in the car while she shopped. At this time of year, there was no telling who she'd run in to in the store. And it was the Saturday morning before Christmas! Everyone would be at the grocery store.

Keith gave me a warning look that told me all I needed to know. Arguing had gotten us into this mess to begin with. It was not going to get us out.

"You're not going to bicker if I leave you here?" Mom asked.

"No, I promise," Keith said.

"Me too!" I added quickly, deciding to trust whatever Keith was thinking.

Mom shifted into gear when she was satisfied with her parking job and looked at us through the rearview mirror. "Okay, if you say so. I'll leave the car on for you. I'll only be a little bit. Just picking up a few things that I'm missing."

After she left, Keith and I sat in silence for a while. The radio played Mariah Carey's "Santa Claus is Comin' to Town" cheerfully. As the sun blared through the window, illuminating the white snow and blinding me in the eyes, I was forced to turn in

Keith's direction for relief from the sun.

"So…" he started when he saw me turn to him. "How have you been?"

I barked out a laugh. "*That's* what you want to ask me?"

"Well, we haven't had a chance to really catch up, have we?" he asked. "You've been too busy yelling at me."

"I haven't been—" But I stopped myself. I was yelling again—proving him right. And I hated that. How did little brothers bring out the worst in us? "I've been good, I guess."

"You *guess*?"

"I've been going through some stuff, okay? But *don't* tell Mom—or Wendy, for that matter."

"Anything you want to share?" he asked.

I shook my head. "Not really, no. How've you been?"

"Good."

No doubt he clammed up because I did. Now it was my turn to reignite the conversation. "Connor's getting big."

"Yep. Just turned a year."

"Are you and Wendy going to try for another one?"

He turned to the window. "Maybe. We haven't decided."

Right. So he was keeping secrets too. Fair enough, considering I was. We hadn't seen each other in a while. A long while, actually. We didn't need to open up to one another.

Although, truth be told, it would be nice to talk to someone who knew my history. Who knew me in and out. Yet someone who could offer an opinion from an outsider's perspective.

I sighed. "Keith, I'm sorry. This week is going to be a long week if we don't find some common ground. Can we try to put our past in the past and not let it ruin our Christmas? Or Mom's?"

He shrugged. "Yeah, I suppose that's fair. It's only a week, right? We can pretend to like each other that long."

"Whatever makes Mom happy," I said.

We were quiet for the next few minutes. I turned back to the window, closing my eyes and letting the warmth of the sun hit my face. Even though it was only December, my body had been craving contact with the sunshine. Better to soak up the vitamin D while I could.

I opened my eyes when I felt the warmth suddenly disappear and the light abruptly pulled away from my face. Another car had pulled up, but when the driver got out, I stared wide-eyed at who was there.

Lyle Cleveland, my old high school boyfriend. This really was a trip down memory lane.

And here I was sitting in the back seat of my mother's car with my brother while she ran into the grocery store. Humiliating.

I turned toward Keith, who hadn't noticed Lyle and was idly looking out his own window.

From my side, there was a knock on the window. "Linda?"

"Is that guy talking to you?" Keith asked.

I cringed and turned back to my window, debating whether I wanted to make it even more awkward and get out. Of course, that would result in me determining whether it would be appropriate to give Lyle a hug after all these years.

Instead, I stayed in my seat and rolled down the window. "Hey!"

"I thought it was you!" Lyle gave me a big smile.

"Yeah. Just…hanging out with my mother," I said. "She ran inside to get a few things."

To my horror, he leaned down closer to the window and spotted Keith. "Hey Keith."

"Lyle! How've you been?" My brother reached across the seat to give my ex a handshake across me.

Could this interaction get any worse?

"Not bad. Just in town for the holidays and I was given a list of things to get."

Right. So he was probably married, then. Of course he was. How many thirty-nine-year-olds weren't? Basically everyone, except me.

My body gave an involuntary shiver as the wind poured into the car.

"Well, I won't keep you hanging," Lyle said. "It was nice seeing you guys. We should get together, if you have time, while we're all still in town."

"That'd be cool, yeah," Keith said.

"Totally," I added dumbly. When did I ever say *totally*?

Lyle gave a final wave and walked off. I gratefully rolled up my window.

"*Totally*," Keith mocked.

"Don't say anything to Mom, or she's going to ask me a million questions about him," I warned. "Please, Keith!"

He rolled his eyes and settled back in his seat. "I won't."

The trunk suddenly opened as Mom threw her groceries in and slammed it shut with such superhuman strength for an old lady. Then she opened the front door and slid into the driver's seat.

"Okay!" she chirped. "Next stop, we need to get some last-minute gifts for Wendy and Connor, which I'll need your help with, Keith."

We spent the rest of the morning running

errands, stopping at Target, then downtown to get coffee from a local coffee shop. We hit up the post office in Batavia on the way home because the one in Corfu was "in the opposite direction," according to Mom, even though it was only about a two minute drive away from her house.

Old lady logic.

Even though I hadn't been home in some time, I recognized that, after the errands had been done, Mom drove us through the traffic circle and down Route 98. She was heading south, instead of going west back toward her house.

"Uh, Mom, where are you going?" I asked.

"I thought I'd take a joyride," she said.

Keith glanced at the time on his phone. "But it's lunch time. Don't you want to get home to eat? I'm sure Wendy could use the break after having Connor all morning."

"She's a stay-at-home mom who also runs a daycare," Mom responded. "I'm sure she has it under control with only one kid. Besides, Gary is there to help as well."

Keith and I exchanged looks. We both smelled something fishy about this, but neither of us said anything. I had a feeling that Mom would have a response for any question we raised.

Once we hit Alexander, she directed the car

onto Broadway and started heading west.

"She's probably taking this to Route 77," Keith murmured to me in the back seat.

I nodded, although I was skeptical. If Mom wanted to joyride, then why was she taking main routes? If she wanted to get home the fastest way possible, she would've taken the same route we came. She was going somewhere specific.

My thoughts were confirmed when, in Darien, she continued on down Route 20 past the intersection for Route 77.

"Uh, Mom, where are we going?" Keith asked.

"Hush," she said. "I know where I'm going."

Again, my brother and I looked at each other. Anticipation building. Was there a worse punishment she had in mind? Were the scope of her errands bigger than she let on? Was she going to drive us out to the middle of nowhere and force the two of us to work together to get home?

The panicking thoughts subsided when she pulled into a coffee shop in Alden and turned the car off.

"You drove all the way out here for another cup of coffee?" Keith asked.

Mom didn't answer as she got out of the car.

I leaned forward to look through the windshield, which was when I saw who was coming out of the shop.

"Keith!" My arm shot out beside me and smacked him in the arm.

"Ow!" he whined. "What was that for?"

"Look!" I pointed out the window.

His eyes grew wide when he saw what I saw. "Noooo!" He groaned. "She *wouldn't*!"

Mom's smiling face suddenly appeared in the window and I let out an involuntary yelp.

"Linda! Keith!" she called to us as if we were standing fifty feet away. "Come out here and say hello to your brother!"

I took in a deep breath and let it out slowly. "Merry Christmas to us."

We climbed out of the car. Marty was standing near the hood, next to Mom, with his arm around a beautiful woman with sandy blonde hair in a fashionable bob. Both of them had bags with them.

I put on a big smile for Mom's sake. "Marty, hi…" I gave him the big sister hug, fully playing the role now.

"Marty?" he said with a laugh. "Nobody's called me that in years."

"Well, calling my little brother *Martin* is just too weird for me," I told him.

"Keith!" he said when he saw my other brother. "You've gotten *old*!"

He gave a tight smile. "Nice to see you too." The two quickly embraced, more for Mom's benefit, before parting.

"Who's this?" I asked, indicating the beautiful woman, more to change the subject than anything else.

"Oh!" Marty said. "This is Luna. She's my girlfriend."

My eyes widened. Luna was very well dressed, even as she stood in the parking lot of a tiny local coffee shop in Alden. She had a sense of elegance to her that I only ever saw in women in New York. As if paparazzi might jump out at any moment and snap pictures of her to be posted online.

That certainly wasn't going to happen out here.

I extended my hand. "Nice to meet you."

She gave me a limp hand and a tight smile. "Nice to meet you too. You must be the older sister, Linda."

"That's me." What did she mean by *older*? I wasn't quite forty yet. I probably needed to call my hair stylist when I got back to New York and have her touch up my roots.

"Which makes you Keith," Luna said when she offered the same limp hand to him to shake.

"I had no idea Marty even had a girlfriend," Mom said. "So I'm sorry that I wasn't expecting you."

"Yeah, that's my bad for springing her on you like

this," Marty said. "But she had nowhere else to go for Christmas, so I thought, why not bring her home?"

"Of course!" Mom said happily. "We'll squeeze!"

Luna's demeanor seemed to change with Marty's comment, but I decided to take a different opportunity.

"How about we get back in the car and head back to the house?" I suggested. "That way we can all eat and catch up."

We moved around to the sides of the car. Over the roof, Mom called to Luna. "You take the front seat! The three kids can squeeze in the back. Keith, why don't you help your brother with the bags?"

I climbed into the backseat, knowing that as the girl, by default I would be regulated to the middle seat. Didn't matter that I was the oldest.

Keith was the first to climb in after me. "This took a turn I wasn't expecting," he murmured to me.

"Mm-hmm," I muttered back.

Marty got in on the other side, sandwiching me in between my brothers. If I thought it was a tight fit before, I felt like a sardine now. Even more childhood memories of family road trips to Pennsylvania or the Adirondacks came flashing back. We never had enough money for Disney.

Mom started the car up and backed out of the parking spot.

I looked over at Keith and I could instantly tell he was thinking the same thing: this week home for Christmas just got a whole lot worse. Funny how nothing brought you closer to someone like a common enemy.

Chapter 13

My stomach was growling, which was only made worse by the fact that there was a delicious meal sitting right in front of me, slowly cooling the longer it sat there untouched.

We were all seated around the table, ready to eat. Everyone, except Marty and Luna. They had been upstairs basically since lunch. Luna had claimed that she needed to rest, and that was several hours ago. My mind tried not to jump to the things they might've been doing just across the hall from my room.

Connor smacked the tray on his high chair again and emphatically shouted something in gibberish.

"I know, honey," Wendy said beside him. "You're

hungry. But we just have to wait for Uncle Martin." There was an undertone to the way that she talked through her son. With Marty and Luna's arrival, Keith, Wendy, and Connor all had to share a room — something that Wendy was obviously not very happy about.

"Mom, can't we just eat already?" Keith asked. "We've been waiting for, like, ten minutes."

"No." Mom shook her head. "Marty and Luna have had a long day. We can wait for them."

A long day? Marty lived in Alden! That was only twenty minutes away!

But I kept my mouth shut.

"Should we go up and remind them that dinner's ready?" Gary suggested.

Mom glanced to the staircase, then back at the food at the table. Finally, she let out a heavy sigh and said, "Oh, all right." She set her napkin on her plate and was about to get up when we heard footsteps at the top of the stairs. Mom settled back into her seat as Marty and Luna came down the stairs.

"Well!" Marty boomed. "I feel well-rested."

"That makes one of us." I couldn't help myself. It slipped out!

Marty didn't seem to hear me as he and Luna took their seats beside Gary, across from where Keith and Wendy sat, and beside where Connor's high

chair was at the end of the table.

"This looks delicious, Mom," Marty said as he scooted in his chair. Without so much as an apology for making us wait, he picked up his silverware and dug into his food.

I was too hungry to say anything. I followed suit and began devouring my own food.

"So, Marty," Mom started, "tell us how you've been."

He shrugged. "Not too bad. Can't complain."

Keith and I exchanged glances. Everyone knew that Mom was hoping for more than that quick assessment of his life. Then again, I assumed, since Marty lived so close, that he saw Mom often. I never really asked how often they talked when Mom and I chatted on the phone, but the fact that she was surprised by Luna being his *girlfriend* made me believe that even Marty didn't stop by to see Mom, even if he was the one who lived the closest to her.

"Where did you and Luna meet?" I asked, to help the conversation along.

"Oh!" Marty sat back in his chair as he finished chewing. He swatted in Luna's direction. "That's a funny story! I was staying at this hotel downtown — well, more like *crashing*. My friends and I went out for a few drinks, and things got out of hand. Anyway, we decided to get a hotel room instead of trying to

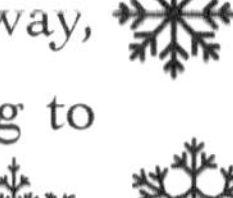

drive back home. So we did, and apparently as each of my buddies woke up, they just left and didn't wake anyone else up. Or maybe they tried, but I was passed out. So when I wake up, the room is empty, I smell like booze, and I feel *real* hungover."

My eyes flickered over to Mom, trying to gauge her take on this story of his. How did he not realize that this painted him in a terrible light and something that Mom would certainly *not* find funny?

"So I decided to take a shower to help myself wake up. Anyway, I get out of the shower, wrap a towel around myself, then figure—what the hell? I'm alone in the hotel room, I don't have to cover up for anybody. And then *bam!* The moment I drop the towel, Luna walks in and catches me butt-naked!"

Mom chuckled politely at that, but I could tell it was forced.

Gary smiled. "Sounds like she got an eyeful."

"I'll say!" Marty went on. "That's not usually the first impression I like to make with a girl. Turns out, I slept right through checkout and since all my buddies left already, she thought the room was empty."

"Are you part of the cleaning staff at the hotel?" Wendy cut into her chicken.

Luna nodded, but didn't say anything else.

"Anyway, I covered up, then asked if she liked

what she saw," Marty went on, casting a devilish smirk in Luna's direction. "We started flirting and I asked if she wanted me to drop the towel again."

"Martin!" Luna said.

He leaned back again and put his arm around the back of her chair. "Nah, I told her I wasn't that cheap and that she'd have to wine and dine me if she wanted another look."

Mom put up her hands to cover her face as she laughed. "Oh, Marty!"

Oh, Marty? That wasn't just some simple boyhood antic. Marty was a grown man!

"Relax, Mom!" he said. "I put my clothes back on and we went on an official date that night."

"One he was *very* well dressed for," she added.

Mom continued to laugh. "I've missed your humor! And I love that you're still the same fun, carefree person you've always been."

Marty sat back and reveled in the compliments. Compliments that he didn't deserve after being absent for so long. Why didn't he ever talk to Mom on a regular basis? Why didn't he ever drop in on her to talk to her? Why didn't he ever think about anyone other than himself?

"How's Dad?" Keith asked suddenly.

Everyone fell silent and all eyes looked over to Mom.

"Keith," Wendy said quietly as a warning after nobody said anything.

"I want to know, too," I added. I knew what Keith was trying to do: poke a hole in Marty's tall tales right from the start. If we were going to spend over a week with him, we certainly weren't going to do it entertaining a lie.

"He's…he's, uh, he's fine," Marty stuttered and turned back to his plate.

"Just fine?" Keith pushed. "What's he up to nowadays?"

"*Keith*," Wendy said with more force.

He shrugged, playing innocent. "What? I want to know. How is dear old Dad? I'm asking the one person who is still really chummy with him. The one who chose our absentee father over the woman who raised three kids on her own. The one who, by the sounds of it, sees that deadbeat more often than the woman who raised us."

Glad that I wasn't the only one who had picked up on that, I added, "You chose the person who abandoned Mom when she was pregnant with you instead of staying with the woman who raised you."

After Keith and I had moved out, Marty had decided that he needed a change too and opted to live with our father, leaving Mom an empty nester much sooner than she had anticipated.

"All right, that's ancient history!" Marty said, that smug smile finally faded from his face. "I'm thirty years old. Can't we just let this go?"

"I don't know, are you ever going to apologize for abandoning Mom?" I asked.

"Like you're one to talk!" Marty fired back. "You got your flashy job in New York City and you haven't been back home since!"

"And yet I still call Mom on an almost *daily* basis," I said. "In fact, I've flown her out to see me at least twice a year since I've been in New York!"

"And how do you know I *don't* see her?"

I crossed my arms and shot him a disbelieving look.

"How could you have the time?" Keith asked. "You spend all your time with Dad—or out partying and flashing the cleaning staff."

Luna stiffened at that.

"Okay, okay!" Gary suddenly roared.

It was the first time, in all the time that I'd known him, that I'd ever heard him raise his voice.

He looked at all three of us with a stern expression. "You all have issues with one another. Fine. Deal with it on your own time. But your mother has asked you here to spend Christmas together and all you're doing is upsetting her."

I looked over at my mother for the first time since

the argument broke out. There were no tears, but it was obvious that she was fighting them back with force.

"Sorry, Mom." I sat on my hands, bringing my shoulders in tighter, feeling about six inches tall.

"Yeah, sorry," Keith added.

"I'm sorry, too," Marty chimed in.

Mom sat quietly, staring down at her plate. When she finally picked up her head to look at us, she said, "Let's all try to have a nice, happy Christmas together. Is that too much to ask?"

Without waiting for a response, she stood and escaped up the stairs.

Chapter 14

After the explosive dinner, none of us felt like spending much time together. We all seemed to recede to our own quiet corners.

Gary had gone up to check on Mom and hadn't been down since. Keith and Wendy were in the bathroom giving Connor a bath. Marty and Luna had gone upstairs to…do whatever they were doing down the hall from Mom and Gary's room.

I didn't want to think about the possibilities.

Still feeling terrible for upsetting Mom like we had, I wanted to be helpful—useful—and I decided to tackle the dishes and clean up the kitchen, since everyone had dispersed before it could be done.

As I worked, I hummed along to Michael Bublé's *Christmas* album, which played over the Bluetooth speakers that were installed underneath the cabinets. I had to give props to Mom and Gary. That was a feature of their kitchen that I hadn't been expecting—when did Mom learn how to use Bluetooth?

Then again, a part of me wondered if she had *ever* used the feature. I could see a salesman of some sort recommending it to them, only for the system to sit unused.

While I worked, Wendy emerged from the bathroom, chasing a naked Connor, who thought it was funny to run away while his parents tried to dress him.

Once they had finally tackled him and gotten him dressed, all three of them sat on the couch and watched a Mickey Mouse show on TV.

I couldn't help but admire their little family. There was only a hint of jealousy in me. Would I ever have that family of three? I thought that by thirty-nine I would've had that by now—maybe a couple more kids, even. And yet here I was, single and childless. At least for the time being. But, as Mom so politely pointed out, my time with childbearing years left was ticking. Would I run out of time before I could have that family I wanted?

D. ALLEN

I finished up the dishes, wiped down the counters, then declared that the kitchen was officially clean. After turning off the Bluetooth speakers, I decided to go upstairs and check some work emails, maybe dive into that book I had started yesterday. Keith, Connor, and Wendy were too comfortable on the couch to try to interfere.

Upstairs, I stopped in my doorway and looked down the hall toward Mom and Gary's room. Their door was closed and I wondered if Mom was crying over what had happened at dinner, letting out everything that she normally kept in check in front of us.

How could we have acted so childish?

I started to turn into my room, when something caught my attention. Voices coming from Marty's room, just across the hall.

Angry voices.

Stepping carefully across the hardwood, I stood just outside of Marty's door so I could hear better. The eavesdropping skills I had developed as a kid apparently never faded.

"…what did you think you were going to do?" Marty asked. "Just sit quiet and blend in with the wall?"

"Of course not, but I didn't expect you to make up such an extravagant story of how we met!"

So it was a lie. Not that I was surprised.

Marty's voice was quieter, so I couldn't make out what he said next. Both of their voices had dropped to a point where I couldn't hear them.

I looked behind me toward the staircase, where I knew that at any moment, Keith and Wendy could come up with Connor to put him to bed. How much longer could I sit here and listen without getting caught?

I started to turn back to my room when I heard Luna's voice.

"We are *not* sharing a bed."

So not everything was picture perfect between Marty and Luna. I had mixed feelings about that. On one hand, I was happy that his life wasn't as perfect as he let on. On the other, I wished my baby brother could find a woman he could settle down with and live a happy life.

Not that I'd found that myself, but I could wish that for others too, right?

"That's what we kind of implied when you agreed to come home with me," Marty told her. His voice was loud. He must've been standing right on the other side of the door.

"You can't force me to."

"What are you going to do?"

"I could blow the whistle on everything you're

telling them," she said.

The stair treads creaked at the bottom, indicating that Keith and Wendy were on their way up with Connor. I scooted into my room and shut the door, pressing my back against it.

It wasn't until I was in the privacy of my own room that I realized that my heart was pounding. Something was up about Marty and Luna, but how was I going to find out what it was without upsetting my mother and ruining her Christmas?

SUNDAY,
December 21st

Chapter 15

My morning started off great. I woke up feeling refreshed and rejuvenated, not to mention excited that there were only a few days left until Christmas.

And then I walked downstairs and was greeted by noise, as if it *wasn't* seven o'clock in the morning.

The TV was on, playing Mickey Mouse, while Wendy sat beside Connor, who was very engrossed in the show. Mom and Gary were both seated at the dining room table with Luna, who was clearly sitting as far away from them as possible. As usual, Mom was already dressed for the day in yet another Christmas sweater. Meanwhile, the rest of us were still in pajamas—or, in

Marty's case, what passed for pajamas.

He wore black sweatpants that sat low on his hips. He was drinking a glass of milk in front of the open refrigerator door. Oh, and he wasn't wearing a shirt.

Who did he think he was trying to impress? We were all family.

Suppressing my annoyance at the overstimulation of the full house, I dragged my feet into the kitchen where Keith stood at the counter, waiting for his toast to pop.

"There's some more coffee if you want it," he offered. The olive branch my mother was so desperately hoping for.

"Thanks."

Keith and I wouldn't need a lot of convincing to mend fences. Not when we had a shared disdain for Marty, who continued to act as if everything in the world was for him and about him.

"Hey, can I have one of those?" he asked Keith, looking over his shoulder into the toaster.

"There's only two pieces of bread in there," he replied. "So no. They're both mine. I can put two more pieces in there when this pops, if you want."

I opened the cabinet and surveyed the options for mugs. There was the chipped green mug that leaked down the side if you didn't drink it at the right angle.

There was the #1 Coach mug, which must've been Gary's contribution. And there was the Best Mom Ever mug, which was a Mother's Day gift from me. I paused as I looked at it, hesitating before taking it.

"Thanks!" Marty said to Keith. He reached around me for a mug, taking the #1 Coach one my hand was reaching for, then filled it with the last of the coffee from the pot.

"Hey!" I said. "That was for me!"

He shrugged. "Getting slower in your old age, aren't you?"

The hits just kept on coming, didn't they?

I sighed heavily.

"Just make another cup," Marty said as he poured entirely too much sugar into what was supposed to be *my* cup of coffee. No way I was drinking it now.

I grabbed a glass from the cupboard and filled it with water. "I need to lay off the caffeine anyway."

Keith finished buttering his toast and carried it on a plate around the counter, balancing his coffee mug in the other hand. Marty made a quick dive in front of Keith for a piece of his toast, which caused Keith to stop quick, sloshing his hot coffee all over his shirt.

"Ow!" He set the mug and the plate on the counter. "What the hell, Marty?"

"Keith, I'm sure he didn't mean it," Mom said

halfheartedly from the table.

"Sorry," our little brother said. "I just wanted some toast."

Keith gestured over to the toaster. "I made you some toast!"

"But yours was already made."

"Is that how Dad operates his house?" I muttered as I handed Keith a wet towel. "Survival of the fittest?"

"Linda…" Mom said in a warning tone.

Marty's fun mood darkened at that. "I guess I would know, considering that I'm the only one who sees him."

"That's because he walked out on us," I said.

"Maybe he couldn't stand you, either," Marty snapped.

Keith finished wiping up the counter, but then got an idea. He handed the wet towel to Marty, who was happily munching on Keith's toast.

"Clean it up." Keith point to the floor.

Marty scrunched his face and, with a mouthful, said, "No! It's not my mess."

Luna tapped him on the arm and turned to mutter something to him, only for her to quickly realize she didn't have his attention.

"*You* made me spill it all over." Keith pulled his shirt away from his body with his fingertips.

"Boys, don't argue," Mom said from the dining room table. She got up and came around the counter into the kitchen. "Keith, go change your clothes, Marty, go eat your breakfast—"

"*My* breakfast!" Keith said.

"Linda, help me clean this up," Mom continued, despite Keith's interruption.

"Me?" I asked. "Why should I clean it up? I wasn't even involved!"

"You had to make that quip about your father," she said.

"And Marty had to act like an entitled, immature *brat*," I shot back. "But he gets a free pass?"

"Hey! All I was doing was getting my breakfast!" Marty called over. He had taken a seat at the dining room table across from Gary.

"*My* breakfast!" Keith corrected.

Wendy came into the kitchen. "I'll help you clean it up, Suzanne." She grabbed another towel from where it hung on the oven and got down on her hands and knees with Mom and started wiping up the spilled coffee.

Now I felt bad. Wendy had been even less involved than I had, but she had the rational mind to be the bigger person. I might've accused Marty of acting like an immature brat, but I wasn't acting much better.

So I found myself grabbing a roll of paper towels and joining Mom and Wendy on the kitchen floor, wiping up the mess that the boys had made.

Life was so unfair.

By the time we were done, I helped myself to the toast Keith had put in the toaster for Marty, now long since popped. It had gone cold, and the butter didn't really melt on the bread. Still, I brought it over to the table and sat beside Gary, who was still sipping his coffee and reading the paper, as if a brash of immature fighting by adult siblings happened in his house every day. I wished I could be that calm.

At the other side of the table, Marty and Luna sat quietly, both of them munching on their own breakfasts—or, in Marty's case, Keith's breakfast.

The cold toast helped settle my stomach, which had been feeling off since I had woken up. That had been happening a lot lately. Usually it passed after I ate something, although this was a far cry from my usual breakfast fare.

Keith came back downstairs in a fresh T-shirt, which was when Marty got up from the table and handed Keith the plate back.

"Here, you can have this back," he said. "Oh, and Linda ate the toast you put in the toaster."

Keith looked at me with annoyance.

"For what it's worth, it's not even good," I told him.

Keith groaned and tossed the plate in the sink with a loud clatter, causing Connor to begin crying on the couch. Keith started to head in the direction of his son, but Wendy, who was sitting right next to Connor, scooped him up before Keith could even take one step. She gave him an annoyed look just before turning toward their son and trying to calm him.

Keith leaned his hands on the counter and lowered his head, feeling defeated.

"You've upset him," Marty said.

"You know, everything was fine until *you* showed up!" Keith spat.

Mom came out of the laundry room by the kitchen. "Boys! Knock it off!" She swatted Keith, who was closest to her, with a towel. "What did I tell you last night about the arguing? It's barely been twelve hours and here you are doing it again! Am I speaking French, or do you understand the words coming out of my mouth?"

The boys sobered at her scolding.

"Sorry Mom," they both murmured in unison.

Mom looked between the two of them. "We're all going to have *fun* today, whether you like it or not. Got it?"

Forced entertainment. That was the spirit of the holidays!

Chapter 16

It was funny how, even though we were all adults, a little scolding by our mother went a long way. After our sibling argument that morning over breakfast, Mom had us sitting around a table decorating cookies as she pulled them out of the oven.

I manned the red frosting—really, it was pink, but it was the closest we could get with food coloring—while Keith used the green frosting. Wendy sat Connor in his high chair next to them, and he very quickly had green frosting all over his face.

That helped relieve the tension because Marty—who was in charge of the white frosting—was grumbling and complaining about the mess, and the level of sugar, and how his cookies didn't look as good as the rest of ours. Basically, he was pouting that he didn't excel at something.

"Ugh, this isn't *working*!" Marty threw his cookie back on the table. Rainbow sprinkles spilled all over the wax paper.

"Relax, Marty," Mom told him. "You're doing great!"

"No, I'm not! This is stupid! And I'm not even going to eat them."

She scoffed. "Oh, it's Christmas! They don't have to be perfect. Cut yourself some slack!" She came over to inspect Marty's work. "This looks great! What are you complaining about?"

"This looks like an eight-year-old did it!"

"So what? Who's going to know?"

"We'll know," Keith said with a snicker.

Mom gave a quick, hard slap to the back of his head. "Don't start, Keith." She turned back to Marty. "Honey, these cookies are for us. And, at the end of the day, they all taste the same. This is supposed to be fun."

She looked over to the living room. Gary had fallen asleep in his recliner. The sounds of the Peanuts Christmas album must've knocked him out. Meanwhile, Luna sat on the couch and flipped through fashion magazines that she had brought with her.

"Luna, honey, do you want to join us?" Mom

asked. "This is a family affair, whether my husband knows it or not."

"I'm all set, thank you," she said politely.

"Suit yourself." Mom sat at the table and watched us.

"You're not going to pull out your camera, Mom?" I asked.

"No, I think I'll just watch."

"But you're *always* taking pictures at Christmas," Keith added.

"I just want to enjoy the moment right now, is that so bad?"

"No, but it's not like you," Marty added. "You're the one who slipped and fell in the melted snow at my basketball game in seventh grade because you were trying to get a closer shot of me *walking into* the gym."

I laughed, remembering it. "Oh my gosh! I forgot abut that!"

"Didn't they call in the paramedics?" Keith asked.

"Had to," Marty said. "The school didn't want to get sued."

Mom scoffed again. "I wouldn't have sued!"

"But it was within your right," Marty said. "We could've been making cookies in a mansion now, if you had only thought to limp a little afterward."

"Were you okay?" Wendy asked.

Mom waved it off. "Oh, I was fine! The only thing that I bruised was my pride."

"Kind of like the time we tried to go ice skating at Christmas and Linda couldn't keep her legs under her," Marty said.

Keith burst out laughing. "Her legs looked like they were made of Jell-O!" He stood back and did a motion similar to the Charleston dance, wiggling his legs back and forth. Through tears of laughter, he added, "She couldn't keep them straight to save her life!"

"Hey! That was my first time ice skating!" I protested. I looked over and saw that even Mom was smirking, which helped me accept the fact that I could be the butt of a story at least once. If I was going to dish it out, I needed to be able to take it too.

"We had good times growing up," I murmured. "You made it fun, Mom."

"Yeah," Marty echoed.

Keith nodded.

"I'm glad you kids thought so," Mom said. "A lot of times it felt like I was barely holding it all together."

We all fell silent as her unspoken words took effect. Our trip home this year must've felt like she was still trying to hold it all together, and my brothers and I all felt a little guilty at that thought.

I grabbed a cookie from the wax paper and held it

up. "How about a toast?"

"With a cookie?" Keith asked.

"It's eleven o'clock in the morning, I'm not popping a bottle of champagne right now," I said.

Marty groaned. "All this sugar. I'm going to have to go for a run later."

I rolled my eyes. "Just do it."

"So motivational," Marty murmured.

"Yeah, you should run for office with that motto," Keith added.

"Boys, give her a chance to talk," Mom said.

Both of my brothers raised a cookie, as did Wendy and my mother.

"Thank you." I stood and addressed the whole table, raising my cookie up proudly. "Here's to a week of trying to relive the happy Christmas memories we had as kids." I looked over at my mother. "I think we all agree that we owe all of those moments to you, Mom."

I could see tears in her eyes. She raised the cookie high and cheered, "Hear hear!"

My brothers clunked their cookies next to mine, as did Wendy, and we each took a bite.

A common enemy might've brought people closer, but nothing worked quite the same as a group of siblings trying to show their mother that they love her.

Chapter 17

I rolled around in my soft white sheets as the city streetlights created shadows around my room.

I was back in my apartment in New York. Weird. I didn't remember traveling back. Was it still Christmas time? Had I dreamed of my trip back to Mom's house?

The sound of a baby crying pulled me back to reality—or rather, this version of reality. Where did the baby come from?

It didn't matter. The baby was upset. Worse, I knew I had nothing to help soothe it.

I tossed the sheets back and stepped across the creaky hardwood toward the sound of the crying. There was a bassinet in the corner of my bedroom, as if it had always been there.

I carefully walked up to it, trying to figure out a plan as to *how I would calm the baby's crying before the neighbors called the super.*

Only, when I peered inside the bassinet, there wasn't a baby there. It was only a black hole. A wormhole, where dreams and hopes and youth went to die. I felt the pull as it began to suck me in.

My eyes snapped open and the first thing I noticed was that I was back in my bedroom at my mother's house. That stupid nightlight that she insisted on glowed brightly enough to allow me to see the outlines of the furniture.

The next thing I noticed was that the baby crying continued. Only, this time, it seemed to come from farther away. Downstairs.

I laid in bed and listened. Connor was inconsolable. I heard Keith and Wendy's voices downstairs, both of them seemed agitated, as I would be if I was woken up in the middle of the night from a peaceful sleep. Then I heard footsteps pounding up the stairs and, from down the hall, a door slammed shut.

I sat up, pulled on a bathrobe, and opened the door into the hallway. Just a crack at first, just to see who else might be there.

Keith and Wendy's door was closed, and yet I still heard crying downstairs and my brother's attempts to soothe my nephew.

Wendy must've reached her limit and tapped out.

I padded down the stairs, where the Christmas lights on the tree and adorned around the windows still glowed, giving a warm, inviting light to the living room that was in complete contrast to the distress of Connor's cries.

"Do you want any help?" I asked quietly.

Keith whirled around, surprised to hear my voice. He was in a plain white T-shirt and plaid pajama bottoms. His hair stood on end in the back. A picture of complete disarray.

He looked at me, then back at Connor, as he tried rocking him back and forth. Finally, he sighed and asked, "Would you mind?"

"Of course not." I wiggled my fingers toward myself as I stepped forward. "Let's see if Aunt Linda has what it takes." It was the first time I had attributed that title to myself. I liked the way it sounded.

Keith passed him off to me and I immediately felt my nephew's tears press against my cheek as his warm clammy body lay against my chest. My heart melted to a puddle on the floor.

Very softly, I rocked back and forth and shushed him, talking in a calm, soothing voice that I had seen done thousands of times before but hadn't done since Marty was a baby. Of course, this was completely

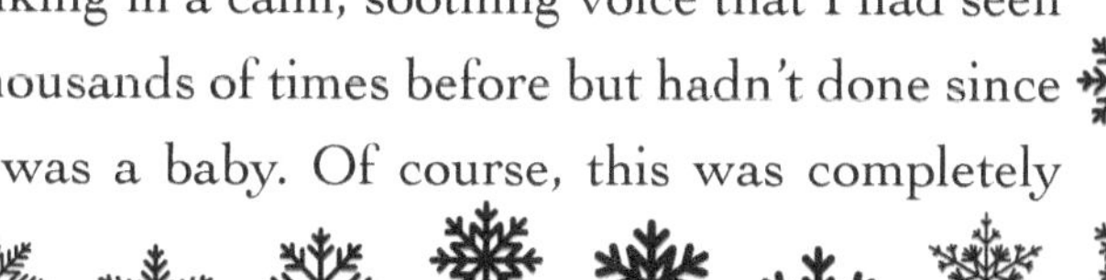

different than being the *almost* ten-year-old big sister taking care of my little brother.

Connor's sobs subsided, but he still wiggled and moved around, which put a strain on my arms and back. How did parents carry their kids for so long? Still, I kept my position and continued rocking in order to calm him.

"Here, I can take him back," Keith said.

I passed him off, and Keith settled into the couch as Connor collapsed into his chest.

I sat on the other end of the couch and watched as father and son both calmed their nerves with the comfort of one another.

There was my heart making a mess again.

"What?" Keith asked after a few minutes.

I shrugged and let a smile creep onto my face. "Nothing. I'm just surprised by your patience."

"Well, if I didn't have any, he would never calm down," he reasoned. "He doesn't really give me much of a choice."

"Still, even Wendy got frustrated and had enough."

"I've had my moments, too," he said. "She's just…this house isn't as relaxing for her as it is for me."

I shrugged again. What part of this trip home was *relaxing* for any of us? "I get that. But still, watching

you become a father, and do it *well*…I'm impressed. And very proud. You're great with him."

Connor began snoring quietly against Keith's chest.

"Thanks," Keith said. "I appreciate that. Is Mom still on your case about having a family?"

"Oh, you know…" I looked down at my bathrobe, which I felt suddenly needed to be straightened out, despite the frumpy middle-of-the-night look. "It was the first thing she mentioned when she picked me up at the airport."

"She just wants you to be happy."

"Which implies that I'm not happy already."

"*Are* you happy?"

I looked away again. "I don't know."

We sat in silence for a moment.

"Look, I'm not going to pry into that with you," he said after a while. "I'm too tired and you're not in the mood to talk about it. All I'll say is this: if you're not really happy, you should do something about it. I've got your back."

I smiled. "Thanks."

He gripped the arm of the couch while holding Connor with his other hand. "All right, I should get this one back to bed." He launched himself to his feet, stumbling a little until he steadied himself, then headed for the stairs. "Thanks for your help. See you

in the morning."

"Good night," I called to him.

After they were gone, I sat on the couch and stared at the tree. *Was* I happy? Or was something missing?

The Christmas lights clicked off after another few minutes, which told me it was time to go upstairs. Whatever was afflicting me, I wasn't going to figure it out in the middle of the night.

MONDAY,
December 22nd

Chapter 18

I didn't know if I was going to make it. Sure, Manhattan was cold, but this was almost downright brutal the way the cold wind slapped against face as my brothers and I walked down the sidewalk. The bakery had never seemed this far before, certainly not by car.

"Whose idea was it to get coffee at the bakery?" I asked loudly, over the wind.

"Yours," both of my brothers shouted in unison.

"Oh. Right. Well, whose idea was it to *walk*?"

"Also yours," Keith said.

Marty scrunched up his face. "It's not that far, guys. You're so car-dependent." He pitched his voice up to a

nasally, whiny voice to mock me.

"Okay, okay, I get it."

We reached the door and Keith was the first to open it. I stepped to the side, figuring he would hold it open for me, but nope. He cut in front of me, beating me inside before I could step into his way. And when I took a moment to look at him with dismay, Marty did the same, leaving me out in the cold.

Did the chivalry end because I was their sister, or were Wendy and Luna missing out on some bygone gentlemanly qualities?

I quickly recovered and joined them inside.

The bakery was small, but it was cute. Farmhouse-style decorations lined the walls, almost to the point of being too much, but it fit the vibe of the little restaurant and all of Corfu, for that matter.

The counter and preparation area seemed to take up most of the space, but there was plenty of room still to sit at the large table in the middle of the dining area. In fact, the table looked like it was pulled straight from somebody's own dining room.

My brothers were already at the register, looking up at the chalkboard on the wall that displayed the menu.

"Everything looks so good here." I surveyed the baked goods, spread out behind glass.

"Will that be all?" the server asked Keith. He was an older man with a scraggly gray beard and wire-rimmed glasses.

He looked over at me. "What do you want?"

I waved him off. "I can get it."

Marty rolled his eyes. "Stop the big sister crap and let him pay for your food."

"Just because you have no qualms about mooching off other people doesn't mean I need to do the same," I snapped.

Keith gestured to the server. "Linda, please. He's waiting."

The server didn't seem to be interested in entertaining our bickering.

I sighed as I looked up at the board. "I'll try some of your lemon tea, and a blueberry muffin."

"Is that everything?" the server asked.

Keith nodded. "Yes. Otherwise, I'll be buying snacks for anyone who walks in."

Marty sat at the table. "Better snag this before the crowd comes in." It was a crack at how few people the place had, but I gave it no attention.

I walked over to take a seat at the table when the door opened again, ushering in the cold winter chill.

"Why hello." Lyle Cleveland looked at me with a big smile. "We meet again."

"In Corfu, of all places," I said.

"Lyle?" Marty jumped to his feet and gave my old boyfriend a big hug, which Lyle hadn't been expecting.

"Oh, hey."

"It's been a while, man!" Marty said.

"Marty!" Keith called from the counter. He nodded in his direction and my youngest brother stepped away to join him, giving me and Lyle a tiny bit of privacy.

"I didn't expect to see you here," he said. "Are you guys staying with your mom?"

I nodded. "She kind of sprung it on us. Lied. Cheated. Schemed. You know, all that holly jolly stuff of the season."

He laughed. "Sounds like something my mom would do too."

Our eyes met and the way he lingered told me that he wanted to have a longer conversation but he hadn't been expecting to run into me. I hadn't been expecting it either.

Marty came back to the table and plopped down in his chair. "Lyle, why don't you join us?"

Another thing stopping me and Lyle from having a real conversation? The circumstances.

It was almost a shame I had to go back to New York in a week.

"Well, I just came in for coffee," Lyle said.

"Mom's actually waiting for me in the car. We're heading out to Hamburg to look at lights."

"In the middle of the day?" I asked.

He shrugged. "She figured with the snow it would look nice. Never mind the fact that I'd have to drive out to the snow belt."

"That's my neck of the woods nowadays," Keith said as he walked over to join us. He shook Kyle's hand—a much more appropriate response to seeing my old boyfriend. "Nice seeing you again." 

"Nice seeing you too," Lyle said. His eyes found mine. "All of you. I'm just going to order some coffee and get out of your hair." 

I took a seat across from Marty as Lyle walked up to the counter. The three of us sat quiet while Lyle ordered. 

I tried to distract myself with other things. The way the snow was coming down outside, it was a wonder the bakery was open at all. But I was grateful it was. I wanted to talk to my brothers in private. Somewhere where we wouldn't have distractions. 

And running into Lyle was nice too.

"It was nice seeing you guys," Lyle said as he walked out with two coffee cups in his hands. He raised one, in an attempt to wave, then used his back to push open the door as he exited, sending in another chill to the bakery. 

"Will you be sneaking out of your bedroom window later, like you used to do?" Marty asked me.

I rolled my eyes. "No. I'm the only one in the house who will be sleeping alone."

Marty shrugged. "Who said anything about sleeping."

Keith made a disgusted face, then quickly changed the subject. "All the stuff we ordered was pretty cheap, considering what we got."

"That's good," I said.

"Maybe we can try to come again sometime before we all leave," Marty suggested.

"About that," I started, "I wanted to talk to you two about this week. I know we've been bickering and sniping at each other a lot—"

"That's because you're too critical," Marty cut in. "I've been trying to enjoy my Christmas but—"

"Here are the drinks." The server set coffees in front of Keith and Marty, and a cup of tea in front of me. He motioned over to a station by the door. "Cream and sugar are right over there."

Marty immediately jumped up and grabbed a handful of sugar packets.

"Grab me two creams," Keith told him. "And I'm stealing one of your sugars. You really don't need that much."

"It's energy!" Marty settled back in his seat and

tossed Keith the cream cups.

"But the sugar cookies we made yesterday weren't?" he asked.

"That's just straight sugar." Marty shook three packets before ripping off the tops of all of them and pouring them into his coffee.

"And the literal *sugar packet* you're putting into your coffee *isn't*?" I asked.

He shrugged. "It's not really sugar. This is the fake stuff."

"It's still—" I put up my hands and stopped myself. There was no use arguing with him. "Never mind. This is exactly what I wanted to talk to you guys about."

"Marty's sugar intake?" Keith stirred his own coffee.

"No, we need to tone it down," I said. "The digs and the bickering and the yelling—it's bringing Mom down."

Keith nodded. "I noticed that too."

"You're both going to have to stop pissing me off then," Marty cut in.

Both Keith and I glared at him.

"Look, I'm not saying we *actually* need to get along." I played with the tea bag, bouncing it in my cup to release the flavors. "We have issues with each other and we're all grown adults with separate lives."

I looked over at Marty and amended my statement. "Or rather, we're two adults and one man-child."

"Oh, so we should follow your example on how not to snipe at each other?" Marty asked. "Good job, Lin."

I sipped my tea carefully. "You're right. I'm sorry. That was…that was an old habit, I guess. But that's my point. We need to fight those natural urges to yell at each other so that Mom can have a good Christmas. After all, that's why we're all here, isn't it?"

Keith shrugged an acknowledgment. Marty nodded slowly.

"You think we'll be able to pull this off?" Marty asked. "Mom asked me to stay until New Year's."

Keith nodded. "Us too."

"And me three," I said. "She knew what she was doing when she invited us separately, which is why she didn't tell us we were *all* coming. And now that we're here, the first thing we do is argue?" I shook my head. "We're letting her down."

"So what do we do?" Keith asked.

"We play nice, even if it's just for this week," I said. "Even if we have to pretend."

Neither of them looked convinced.

"All right," the server said as he returned. "Here's the food. One cup of hot soup, one chocolate scone,

and one blueberry muffin."

I looked over at Marty, who got the chocolate scone, and wanted to make a comment about how his food choices were in contradiction to his complaints about what we had been eating, but I bit my tongue. If we were going to pretend to be nice to each other, I needed to start right away.

After the server left, I said, "Think about yesterday when we were making cookies."

"And Marty threw a fit because his weren't perfect?" Keith said.

"Hey!" Marty called out.

"Guys!" I said, feeling like a referee. "This is what I'm talking about. We need to stop with all of this. Sure, yesterday we were bickering, but then we remembered some happy stories and we were getting along without even trying. We need to try to focus on that so that we can give Mom a happy Christmas."

"Do you think something's up with Mom?" Keith asked.

"What do you mean?" I asked.

He shrugged, then waved it off. "Never mind. It's probably nothing."

"Then why would you say that?" Marty smacked his lips, sucking up the scone crumbs that had stuck to his fingers.

"It's just…I felt like Gary was trying to tell me

something the other night while we were cleaning up from dinner," Keith said. "But he was probably just trying to make conversation. We don't really have anything in common."

I nodded. That much was true. Gary seemed more like an unfamiliar friend of Mom's and it took effort—at least on my part—to remember that he was actually her *husband* and was, technically, part of the family.

"Regardless," I pressed, "can we agree to at least *pretend* to be nice to each other?"

Both of my brothers looked at each other.

"Come on!" I said. "We used to do it all the time when we were younger and wanted something."

Keith laughed. "Yeah, we got pretty good at manipulating Mom, didn't we?" He glanced over at Marty without a word.

"Hey!" our little brother whined.

"I didn't say anything," Keith said.

I sat back and sighed, but caught the glimmer of humor on my brothers' faces. This was going to be harder than we thought, but I had a good feeling that we could do it.

Chapter 19

I had to admit, I was starting to finally relax. Mom's house was foreign and familiar, all at the same time. And after Keith, Marty, and I all agreed on a truce, the underlying tension we had all felt had dispersed as well.

I was sitting on the couch reading my book while Luna sat on the other end, flipping through her magazines. Gary had fallen asleep in his recliner. Mom was down in the basement doing laundry and Keith and Wendy had gone upstairs to "nap."

Gross.

I thought my brother would be able to hold off while he was home for Christmas, but I guess not.

Marty lay on his stomach on the floor, playing with Connor. Our little nephew held one of his colorful toys in his tiny fist and gnawed on it. He could pull himself up on his own, but he was still unstable, so Marty held his hands at the ready to catch him in case he fell. He grabbed one of Connor's feet and blew on the bottom of it with his lips, which caused laughter to erupt from the tiny toddler.

It was actually very cute, watching my little brother—the same one who always had such bravado—being goofy and silly to try to make Connor laugh.

Mom came up the stairs from the basement with her laundry basket and set it on the dining room table with effort. She sounded out of breath.

"Do you need help with that?" I offered.

Mom closed the basement door and shook her head. She was trying to play off her breathlessness. "No, I'm okay. I've been doing laundry for years!"

I wasn't convinced, but I let it slide.

Mom came to stand behind the couch, leaning on the back of it for support, and smiled as she watched Marty and Connor on the floor by the Christmas tree.

"Aren't you going to snap a picture?" I asked.

"No." Mom shook her head. "Just enjoying the moment."

Add that to the list of things that seemed off about

Mom. But again, I didn't say anything.

Mom nudged Luna, who didn't seem particularly interested in the cute moment that held everyone else's attention. "Can I plan on you and Marty giving me another grandchild?"

"Mom!" Marty snapped.

"Actually, Martin and I—" Luna started, but Marty scooped up Connor and quickly rose to his feet.

"Luna and I haven't discussed kids yet, Mom," he said quickly. "So I'd rather you not pressure us about it."

Mom put up her hands in surrender. "Okay. I get it. Touchy subject."

Marty and Luna glared at each other, and suddenly the tension that I thought had been lifted was back again.

I got back to my feet. "I'm going to read my book upstairs." Quickly, I raced up the stairs to escape whatever awkwardness was about to fill the living room. I was about to head into my room when I heard angry hushed voices coming from Keith and Wendy's room.

"…whenever we can," Keith said. "This seems like a good opportunity."

"It doesn't matter," Wendy said. "It's not going to work anyway."

I was getting good at this eavesdropping thing. I remembered doing it when we were kids, until Marty caught me the time he had stolen fireworks from the neighbor after a Fourth of July party. Even though he had the contraband fireworks, *I* was the one who got in trouble for snooping.

So this time I was extra careful, looking down the hall in case anyone came upstairs, and mapping out my exit plan and excuse for being right outside Keith and Wendy's door if they were to suddenly step into the hallway.

"Well, it's certainly not going to with that attitude," Keith said to Wendy on the other side of the door.

"How else am I supposed to feel?" she asked. "It's been months and nothing's worked."

"And if we don't try right now, it'll only be another month before we can try again."

I placed a hand on my own belly and started to step away. This was too personal of a conversation for me to listen in on. The hurt in Wendy's voice was evident, and while I had no issues with violating Keith's privacy, I didn't want to cross that line with Wendy.

"Do you think I want this stress on me at Christmas?" she asked.

"What difference does it make?" he said, louder.

"You never want to think about it."

I hurried to my door, but didn't have time to close it before their door swung open. Wendy marched down the hall, paying me no mind as she descended the stairs.

Keith, however, saw me.

I looked at him, feeling guilty for overhearing their private conversation. "Is everything okay?"

"How much did you hear?" he asked.

I looked down at my book in my hand, ashamed at being caught. "Enough to know you guys were arguing."

It was no relief to learn that Keith and Wendy were not, in fact, the perfect couple that Mom had always made them out to be. The only ones who had given her a grandchild and had "settled down."

My brother turned his vitriol toward me. "Next time, mind your own business, would you?"

"Keith, I'm sorry!" I followed him back into his room. "But since I overheard…do you want to talk about anything?"

"You're just looking for the gossip." He fixed the corners of the bed, which had been made to perfection and required no further fussing. Clearly, it hadn't been slept in—or any other acts.

"Not at all." I sighed. "Keith, I meant what I said yesterday when we were making cookies. I *want* to

relive the happy memories of our childhood. And what I remember is that you and I were actually pretty close. We were the older ones. The ones Mom kind of let do our own thing when Marty became too much of a handful. We trusted each other. So trust me now."

He stood there, with his hands on his hips, and stared at the floor. "Wendy is having a hard time getting pregnant again."

"Oh." The snippets of the conversation that I'd overheard suddenly made sense.

"Yeah."

"Well, it doesn't always happen right away, from what I've heard…" I offered, even though I knew it wasn't much help. As if Keith and Wendy didn't already know that.

"Yeah, well, it's been almost a year that we've been trying and still nothing. It's weighing on her because she feels like she's doing something wrong, which of course isn't true, but I can't convince her of that. My attitude is that we need to keep trying, but when she's taking on all of the stress of expanding our family, it doesn't really put her in the right mindset to…well, you know."

We were approaching the limits of my ability to talk about my brother's sex life, so I rerouted the conversation.

"Wait, you said you've been trying for almost a year?"

"Just about," he said.

"Didn't Connor just turn a year old not that long ago? How long after he was born did you two start trying?"

He shrugged. "Pretty quickly. Wendy got it in her head that she wanted the kids to be close in age, so we started trying right away."

"Still, that's *really* close." Hadn't Wendy seen the way my brothers and I had been at each other's throats since we'd all arrived? Didn't that deter her from wanting more kids?

"Yeah, we knew it'd be hard, but Wendy is a stay-at-home mom and she wants to get back to work eventually, which means we need to have the kids sooner so they can start school around the same time in a couple years."

I nodded. "Okay." That sounded plausible. "But still, that's a, uh…very *aggressive* plan."

"Well, it's not working anyway, so what does it matter?" He threw his arms up and turned away.

Time to change my approach. "Have you seen anyone about this? Like a doctor or someone?"

He crossed his arms. "I've brought it up, but Wendy's not there yet. I think that would only stress her out more, admitting that there might be a problem."

"I'm sorry, Keith." I stepped forward and hugged him. He didn't immediately reciprocate, but when I squeezed him tighter, he finally put his arms around me too and squeezed me back.

"Thanks." He held me close, both of us finding comfort in one another.

"On the bright side, at least you have Connor," I said. "He's the cutest thing ever."

Keith nodded. "I know. And I'm grateful for him. I am. But…I don't know, our family doesn't feel *complete* yet, you know? And I think about what life will be like for Connor if he grew up on his own—and he'd be fine and happy—but he'd also miss out on what it's like to have siblings."

"The complicated love-hate relationship that persists into adulthood?" I asked with a smirk. "Yeah, because we're shining examples of healthy sibling relationships."

"I don't know. You said it yourself, we had some good times. And, if I'm being honest, it's nice to be back together this week for Christmas, teasing each other, seeing each other interact with our families."

I smiled and tried not to think about the fact that Keith was technically the only one with a family.

"Yeah, that is nice," I said. "You and Wendy will figure it out. You might need some medical intervention, or you might actually be a complete

family right now without even realizing it. Either way, I'm here for you."

"Thanks." He pulled me in for another hug. Then, as an attempt to make light of our heavy conversation, he ruffled my hair so that it fell all in my face.

"Keith!" I groaned as I stepped away from him and fixed my hair.

"What? I thought you agreed that you liked the teasing?"

I shot him a look.

"Thanks for talking," he said. "Really. I'm glad you're here."

"Of course."

He started to head toward the door, but I stopped him.

"Keith."

"Yeah?"

"When it comes to you and Wendy, maybe you should approach it less as trying again and again until she's pregnant and instead approach it more as you and your wife coming together to…"

There was that limit of my comfort zone again.

"Ah, I got it."

"What it sounds like to me is that she's blaming herself for not giving you the second baby you want, and she's not feeling heard, or loved," I offered. "So

love her first, and let the rest fall into place."

He squinted his eyes. "Did she pay you to say that?"

"Not at all." I flicked my hair over my shoulder. "Just call it woman's intuition."

TUESDAY,
December 23rd

Chapter 20

"All right, so everyone understands the rules, right?" I asked as we walked into the mall. I hadn't been to the Galleria Mall since I was a kid, so walking in was a bit overwhelming as I took in all the sights and sounds of the pre-Christmas chaos. On the bright side, it was Tuesday morning, so it wasn't as wild as it probably had been the previous weekend, but it was still pretty busy.

"Why do we even need to get each other gifts?" Marty asked. "We're all adults. Besides, this time last week, we hadn't spoken to each other in a while."

Keith crossed his arms and looked at our little brother. "You're telling me, when Mom is opening all the gifts on Christmas, that you're not going to be a *little* jealous that you didn't get any?"

"Well…"

"Besides," I added, "we're not just here to get each other gifts. I want to get gifts for Connor and Wendy and even Luna. I can tell she's feeling out of place this week, so maybe some gifts will help cheer her up. Anything in particular she might like?"

"Uh…" Marty stammered, then he giggled. "The things she might like would look awkward coming from you."

I made a face. "Gross."

"We'll find something," Keith said. "But listen, I've been leaving Connor with Wendy a lot since we came home. I don't want to be here all day. Meet back here by noon at the latest?"

I checked my phone. That only left two hours to shop for Keith, Wendy, Connor, Marty, and Luna. Hopefully I'd be able to resist shopping the sales for myself and find something perfect.

I sighed. "Sure. And let's try to stay in the twenty-to-thirty dollar range. There's no reason we need to go broke."

Marty nodded. "Got it. Cheap gifts only."

I gave him a look. "Don't buy junk, Marty."

"Hey, you said stay under twenty bucks, so I'm going to stay under that."

"Twenty per person," I said. "Thirty dollars max."

"Okay, before we lay out even *more* rules," Keith said, "let's just go so we can finish and hopefully be back at Mom's before lunch."

We split up and I watched as both of my brothers went upstairs to shop the stores on the upper level. Hopefully they weren't shopping together. That was also against the rules we had laid out in the car, although I think they had both been tuning me out.

My first stop was Starbucks, where I wasted fifteen minutes in line to get a festive drink. By the time I paid and had my drink in hand, I found a map kiosk to get my bearings of what was even offered in the mall, since it had been so long since I was here last.

I decided to head up to a dollar store first. Connor was only one, so there was no sense in spending a ton of money on him when he wouldn't even remember it. I figured I could find a stuffed animal or some other toy that would be suitable for his age.

Along the way, I passed a maternity store and stopped to look at the clothes in the window. I could see my reflection in the window and I tried to imagine what it would be like to wear some of those clothes. The dream of a nice, happy family like Keith had was just that: a dream. I guess, given Keith and Wendy's troubles to conceive, it was even a dream for them.

At the dollar store, I scored a stuffed animal for Connor and a ring light for Marty—I was sure he probably was very active on social media. I cashed out, picking out some Christmas wrapping paper by the register to add to my order, then headed back out into the mall for the next people on my list.

My mind was blank for what to get everyone. I still had Keith, Wendy, and Luna to shop for.

Keith was an English teacher, so I headed toward the other end of the mall toward the bookstore, but I stopped when I came upon a tiny little chocolate store. I went in, debating whether chocolates would be better suited for Wendy or Luna.

It seemed like a more impersonal gift, meant for someone you didn't know very well, like Luna. But judging how thin she was and how she was constantly looking at fashion magazines, I also didn't picture her enjoying anything with sugar in it. In fact, that was probably why Marty had been complaining about how much sugar was in stuff— not that he had had much self control in the last few days.

That left Wendy. But given what Keith had told

me about how she was having a difficult time lately, I wanted to get her something special. The trouble was, even though Wendy had been my sister-in-law for several years now, and even though we got along pretty well, I didn't really know her. What did she like? What made her happy? How did she spend her days?

Being among the delicious-smelling chocolate, I decided to get a box of sponge candy anyway. If all else failed, I would eat it myself.

I continued down the mall toward the bookstore, but again stopped short when I saw a gift shop. Maybe I could find something for Wendy in there.

It was mostly Christmas ornaments and other novelty things that didn't hold nearly as much value as the prices suggested. Then I saw it, displayed up on the counter by the register in a small cardboard display box, was a small package with a necklace on it. The centerpiece of the necklace was two circles intertwining together, but it was the saying on the package that sealed the deal for me. It said: "Even miracles take time."

I knew it was perfect for Wendy, and I wanted her to have it. Even as I second-guessed whether *I* should be the one to give it to her to respect her privacy, I still wanted her to have it. She needed hope and whether it was me or Keith who gave it to her, I knew this necklace would serve as a helpful reminder to be patient and to let things happen in their own time.

Speaking of time, I checked my phone and saw that I only had thirty minutes left to shop. I hurried down to the bookstore, where I got lost with all of the titles. There were so many books that *I* wanted to read, but I forced myself to focus on Keith. What were some of the books that he liked?

I wanted to text Wendy, but I didn't have her number, so I called my mother instead.

Naturally, she didn't pick up on the first try. The woman was glued to her phone, and yet whenever I needed her she never seemed to answer.

While trying to find Gary's number in my list of contacts, my phone rang. It was my mother.

"Mom! Why didn't you pick up the phone?"

"I was busy playing with Connor," she said. "You know, Wendy's been teaching him sign language and that boy knows how to tell us what he wants! He's so smart. She's doing such a good job with him."

"That's great, Mom," I said flatly, even though I did find it really cool. "Speaking of Wendy, can I talk to her quick?"

"What for?"

"I'll explain later. Just put her on."

In the background, I could hear my mother

calling for my sister-in-law, then a muffled, "Linda wants to talk to you."

"Hello?" There was a hint of confusion in Wendy's voice, mixed with a twinge of worry.

"Hey, sorry. I didn't have your number, otherwise I would've called you. Listen, I'm shopping for Keith and I'm at the bookstore. What kind of books does he want?"

"Oh," Wendy said with a quick laugh to her voice that sounded like relief. "He'll read anything. Usually he gets his books from the library, but he does have a small collection of books. Lately, he's been going for those fancy leather-bound classics. You know, the Tolstoys, the Fitzgeralds, that kind of thing."

I eyed the table across the room with those very books and walked over to it. "Does he have the Charles Dickens collection of Christmas stories? The main one is *A Christmas Carol*."

"No, I don't think he has that one."

"Perfect, thank you! Don't tell him I said anything."

"No problem."

"How is it with Mom?"

"She's actually a big help," Wendy said. "We're going to feed Connor lunch soon and then she even offered to put him down for his nap, so I'm all set here. No need to rush home."

"Awesome. Can you tell Keith that? He's been watching the clock."

"I'll text him. See you later."

"Thanks again, Wendy!"

After I hung up with Wendy, I cashed out at the bookstore, then headed back across the mall to meet Keith and Marty. I expected the two of them to be waiting for me but, of course, I was the first one there.

Finding a bench, I took a seat and felt the relief in my lower back from all the walking, and the ease in the muscles of my shoulders from carrying the bags.

Like anyone in the twenty-first century, I pulled out my phone to entertain me while I waited…

…and promptly saw a text from Keith to me and Marty.

WENDY CALLED. SHE SAID WE HAVE TIME FOR LUNCH. MEET AT THE FOOD COURT?

It had been sent two minutes ago, which meant that he hadn't been waiting long. I gathered my bags, got back to my feet, then headed upstairs toward the food court.

Keith and Marty had already claimed a table, with their bags marking their spot.

"There you are!" Marty said. "It's about time! We've been waiting forever!"

I looked down at my phone, then back at him. "Keith texted less than ten minutes ago. What do you mean you've been waiting?"

Keith rolled his eyes. "He just got here too. Don't let him fool you."

"Dude! Bro code?"

"Dude, she's our sister."

We went our separate ways to order our food, then met up back at the table, all of us with a different variation of fast food.

The Christmas lights and music and ambiance of home was nice, but there was something to be said about fluorescent lights, overspending, and fast food to put you in the Christmas spirit as well.

Or maybe that was only because I never usually took a trip to the mall except at Christmas time.

"So did we all stay within the rules?" I picked at my French fries, which had been paired with the chicken nuggets I had gotten as well, as if I was seven years old. Hey, if I was going to indulge in fast food, then I was going to *indulge*.

Marty nodded. "Sure did." He had found a juice bar and ordered a fruit smoothie for lunch, which, again, had much more sugar in it than he probably realized.

"Good," I said. "I can't wait to see what you got me on Christmas Day."

"That's in two days."

"Which means you better get wrapping when we get home," I said. "Mom is going to have a busy day for us tomorrow. You might not have any time."

Marty's eyes widened. "Oh shoot."

"The *official* Christmas festivities starts tomorrow, first thing in the morning," Keith said. "How could you forget that?"

I reached for another fry. "Although, with the way that Mom has been acting lately, maybe she won't be as crazy."

"You think?" Keith asked.

I shrugged. "I don't know. I don't know what's going on with her. Maybe it's nothing. Maybe *I'm* the one who is acting different."

"Regardless, we're going to be busy tomorrow." Keith sipped from the straw of his fountain drink. Blue liquid came up through the plastic. I was guessing Gatorade.

"I better go to bed early tonight," Marty said. "She's going to have us up first thing tomorrow and not give us a break until we go to bed on Christmas Day."

"Well, in preparation of all that insanity, I'm glad that we had some time to get away, just the three of

us," I said. "I had fun with you guys today."

"Even though we split up when we got to the mall?" Marty asked.

"That was the best part." My smile told him I was kidding.

"I agree," Keith said. "The getting together just the three of us part. I'm actually remembering why I liked you guys."

"Did you, though?" Marty asked.

I raised an eyebrow. "You better hope that he remembered that he liked you when he was picking out your gift. The question is, did you find a gift that's equally as impressive?"

Marty looked worried. "I may need to make a pitstop before we head to the car."

We laughed. It really was nice spending time with my brothers again. I missed them.

Chapter 21

By the time we got back to Mom's house, I was exhausted. Luckily, I had a ready excuse to escape up to my room.

"Sorry! Gotta wrap all these gifts before tomorrow!"

Of course, the plan was to take a twenty-minute nap and *then* start wrapping. Invest in myself before giving to others.

But when I set the bags down on my bed, I heard a knock on my door. It was Marty.

"Hey." He stepped in with his bags before I could even invite him in.

I looked down at his bags then back up at him. "You want me to wrap those for you, don't you?"

"Please?"

I crossed my arms. "What about Luna? Can't you con her into doing it for you?"

"No, she's mad at me for taking so long at the mall this morning."

I made a face as I put myself in Luna's shoes. Of course she was annoyed. She was spending the week with her boyfriend's family, who she hadn't met before arriving, and he ditched her all morning. If that were me, I'd be pissed too.

"Sorry," I said.

"Yeah." He shrugged. "She'll get over it. So, can you help me? And promise to act surprised when you open yours."

I gave him a look. Marty was ruining the Christmas spirit for me for yet another year. But it was fine. I was used to it. Besides, I hadn't been expecting a gift from Marty this year anyway—I didn't even know I'd be spending the week with him—so I could have one surprise spoiled for me. And, if history was any indication, his gift would be something that he found funny and I would later have to find a way to get it off my hands without a serious hit to my conscience.

I held out my hand. "Fine. But you have to help."

His shoulders dropped and he groaned. "Do I have to? You always wrap everything so nicely!"

"Sure, because I've had practice. It's time you start practicing too." I took a seat on the floor and set his bags to the side. I reached up on the bed and pulled out the roll of wrapping paper I had bought on our outing.

Pointing up at the desk, I said, "Find me a pair of scissors and some tape. Oh, and see if Mom has any tags in her room."

"Got it, boss."

He left the room and, just when I thought I was going to have to go out and chase him back to my room to help, he returned with a sheet of sticker tags and a pen.

After he took a seat beside me on the floor, I pulled the first gift out of his bags. It was a little outfit for Connor that read, *My uncle is my favorite.*

My heart melted at the sight and I held it close to me. "Oh, Marty! This is so sweet!"

"Do you think he'll like it?" he asked. "I wasn't sure what his favorite color was, so I went with white. It's pretty neutral."

I decided to avoid popping his bubble by reminding him that white was probably the worst option, considering how much of a mess Connor made when he ate. So instead, I just said, "He's only a year old. He doesn't even have a favorite color yet."

"Perfect!"

Coming back to my senses, I looked down at the outfit. "Damn. We need a box—and some tissue paper." I looked over at him, but he held up his hands in surrender.

"Hey, I already left once to run your errands. If you forgot something, that's on you."

So out I went into Mom and Gary's room to search through the wrapping paper tote for what I needed. Luckily, Mom had everything perfectly organized. I grabbed what I needed, then turned to head back to my room, but stopped short when I noticed the rest of the bedroom. Mom was notoriously organized, to the point of obsession. And yet, everything else in her room that *wasn't* the wrapping paper bin was pretty…sloppy.

Piles of clothes lay against the wall, cups littered the nightstand, and the bed was unmade. If I didn't know any better, I would've thought this was Marty's teenaged bedroom. Or hell, his current bedroom.

By the time I made it back to my room, Marty had pulled out the rest of his gifts and set them in piles around my room.

"You weren't peeking into my bags, were you?" I asked.

"No, Lin. I'm not a Scrooge."

"Funny." I groaned as I settled back down onto the floor beside him. I chose the right sized box for

Connor's little outfit, then pulled out the tissue paper and set it inside. "This is just so the box doesn't look so plain. I usually add two layers, just because it's so thin, but you don't have to—you would just need to be careful not to rip it when you put it in the box."

"Mm-hmm." He was only half-listening, but I still wanted to teach him how to do it on his own. Maybe save myself—or Luna—the job of wrapping his gifts  in the future.

I finished packing up the box, then handed it to  Marty. "All right. I'm doing too much of the work. Now's your turn. Roll out the wrapping paper and  set the box on the sheet. Try to get the same amount on both sides of the box—enough to cover the whole  thing."

"I *know* this part." Without help, he rolled it out  like I had instructed, then cut the wrapping paper— opening and closing the scissors on the paper the  whole way up, leaving jagged edges along the brand new roll. The sight of it was like hearing nails on a  chalkboard.

"If the roll is tight enough, you should just be able  to slide the scissors all the way up," I told him. "It's faster that way, and it leaves a clean cut. But it's not  that big of a deal."

He shot me a look that told me I was being too  picky. This was Marty's gift to a one-year-old, after

all. Aesthetics didn't matter so much.

"Now, you're going to want to make sure the top and bottom are evenly-spaced too," I told him. "And then tape one side and pull it tight before wrapping the other side and taping that tight."

Awkwardly, he followed my directions. I only gave in to my perfectionism a little bit when I reached over and pressed my finger onto the tape he laid out, smoothing it down firmer onto the package.

"All right, these corners are where it gets tricky." I showed him how to do one side. "You want to fold in the sides first, then fold the top and the bottom pieces and, again keeping it nice and tight, tape those closed too." I spoke as I walked him through the steps. Once it looked good, I flipped the package to the unfinished side and said, "Now you try."

He repeated my instructions, to decent success. The folding looked similar to mine, but not as nice and tightly wrapped. But, that came with practice. In the end, the gift didn't look as perfect as I would've liked, but it certainly looked like Marty did it himself.

"Not bad," I told him. "You'll get the hang of it by the time you're done with them all."

He sighed. "Okay. I suppose I should get started." He grabbed another one of his packages and I reached in my bag for what I had bought for

Keith. Might as well get my wrapping done while I helped Marty.

"So, Luna seems nice." I kept my eyes down as I measured out the wrapping paper, then grabbed the scissors and cut what I needed.

"Yeah, she is."

"Is she always quiet?"

He shrugged. "She's just kind of uncomfortable here."

"Yeah, I got that vibe."

His head shot up. "You did?"

"Well, yeah. She doesn't really want to participate in the same things as us. She doesn't say much. She just kind of…sits there and flips through her magazines."

"Oh." He seemed to deflate at that.

"But I'm sure she's glad to be here with you," I offered.

"Maybe." He remained quiet as he struggled to fold the corners the way I had shown him.

After watching him for a few minutes, I pushed him aside and took over. "Here, let me show you."

Marty took the momentary break in wrapping duties to push the scrutiny on me. "So, what's your boyfriend's name? Mom said you were seeing someone."

"When did she say that?"

"I don't know. A couple months ago when we were talking on the phone. He didn't want to come be a part of this madhouse for Christmas?"

I was quiet as I finished wrapping the gift that Marty was supposed to be wrapping himself. I didn't know if I should tell Marty what had happened. Did I trust my little brother with the biggest secret I had ever kept? The truth was going to come out eventually. It always did.

"Actually," I said, "Barry and I broke up. A few months ago."

"Oh, Linda, I'm sorry." Marty did, in fact, look genuinely sorry. "You'll find someone else."

"That's the thing…I'm not sure I'm going to have time."

He looked confused, and then his face softened. "Is this because of what Mom keeps saying about how you only have so many years left to have a baby? Don't let that dictate your life. When you meet someone, you can decide when and how you'll have kids—if you even want them. Mom will have to get over it."

I sucked in a breath. It was now or never. "That's the thing…I'm kind of…pregnant."

His eyes shot up to mine, then down to my belly, then back to my eyes. "You're—you're *pregnant*?"

"Shh!" I stole a glance toward the door. Everyone

else was still downstairs. Hopefully talking or playing the TV or music high enough so that Marty's outburst didn't carry. "Not so loud! Nobody knows!"

"Nobody? You didn't tell Mom or Keith or…?"

I shook my head. "The only other person who knows is my doctor. I'm about eight weeks along. Still early enough to decide if I want to keep it."

"But you don't want to do that, do you?"

I shrugged. "I don't know! I'm kind of scared, Marty. It's not like you, who lives with Dad who can help you if you need it. Or Keith, who lives around the corner from his in-laws. I live six hours away! In a big city, all by myself. And, truth be told, the distance kind of sucks."

"Hey." Marty took my hand, which was a relief that I didn't know I needed. When I looked at him, he said, "You would be a *great* mother. And no matter what you decide, you'll never be alone."

I smiled at him and squeezed his hand. I wiped away the tears that had spilled out. "Thanks, Marty. That means a lot."

"Of course. You're my big sister. I can't let anyone push you around—even yourself." He sat back, giving up on wrapping for the moment. "Now, this boyfriend? I'm assuming he hit the road?"

"We didn't break up because I'm pregnant." Just saying those two words out loud felt freeing. *I'm*

pregnant. "I found out after the fact and he was the last guy I was with, so…"

"Do you want him to be involved?"

"Not necessarily, but he's the father so he has a right to know."

"So you're going to tell him?"

"I kind of have to, don't I?"

He shook his head. "Not alone. When you tell him, make sure I'm there."

"Oh, you're just going to pop over to New York real quick to be there when I tell him?"

"I could move a few things around." He smiled. "I mean it, Linda, I'm here for you. And I'm sure Keith will be too."

"After this week, I know that now. Thank you." I looked over and smiled back at him. "I'm sorry for how much of a hard time I was giving you when you first got here. You really have grown up, and it wasn't fair of me and Keith to hold you up to our previous perceptions of you."

"Thanks. But can I tell *you* a secret?"

"Anytime."

"Sometimes, I still feel like a screw-up too."

WEDNESDAY,
December 24th

Chapter 22

"Luna, honey, are you sure you don't want to help?" Mom called from the kitchen.

Luna sat on the couch, again flipping through a magazine. I couldn't tell if it was the same one that she kept perusing or if she had brought a stack of them with her from home. I thought it was strange reading material to bring on a trip, but everyone found different ways to entertain themselves.

"I'm fine here, thanks." Luna didn't even pick up her head when she called back.

"Would you mind if we put on some Christmas music?" Wendy asked. She had the baby monitor in her hand. Connor was down for a nap.

"Well…" Luna started.

"Find something instrumental on Spotify," Mom said.

My mother's ability to keep up with the technological times surprised me yet again.

Wendy found a playlist and connected to the Bluetooth speakers in the kitchen, then set her phone and the baby monitor on the island, out of the way from the food we were preparing.

As promised, Mom had a busy Christmas Eve planned. The boys were outside shoveling the driveway from last night's snow and the girls and I were inside preparing not just one, but *two* Christmas feasts. One for Christmas Eve and one for Christmas Day. Even though it was the same group of people both days, Christmas Eve itself was its own holiday to our family, dating back to when grandparents and aunts and uncles and cousins used to all come together the day before Christmas. Back before the family got too large and extended to fit into one house, or have any meaningful relationships with each other.

Mom had a hard time lifting the turkey, which left me with my sleeves rolled up, pulling the innards from the fowl's rear-end.

Not my favorite thing to do.

Mom, meanwhile, was preparing the apple pie on

the counter space behind me.

"How can I help?" Wendy asked.

Indicating with her head, Mom motioned toward the fridge. "Could you please pull the rolls out of the fridge? I know everyone likes warm bread, but we're going to be using the oven all day and we need make some priorities. Set the oven to three-fifty."

Wendy pulled a pan from the fridge with the rolls evenly laid out.

"Let me see those," Mom, the Queen of the Kitchen, said.

Wendy held the pan out for her inspection.

Mom nodded her approval. "Good, they all rose nicely."

"How long are those rolls going to take?" I asked from my spot at the sink. I was pretty sure I had finished cleaning out the turkey, but it was hard to tell because the tips of my fingers had gone numb from how cold the inside of the bird was.

"Fifteen minutes at most," Mom said. "Then the pie is going to have to go in, so I need to hurry up and finish this. How's the turkey coming along?"

"I think it's ready to go in the oven."

Mom shook her head in disagreement. "Put it in an oven bag, then set it in one of those aluminum pans I have in the pantry. Wendy, she's going to need help getting it into the bag."

My sister-in-law nodded and went to retrieve the aluminum pan from the pantry. "Where are the oven bags?"

"Top shelf, on the right." Mom was in her element.

"Got it!"

While Wendy and I struggled to get the turkey in the bag, I couldn't help but sing along to the Christmas carols. Even though there were no words to the song, they were the same standards I'd heard my whole life. This was the first time since my brothers had arrived that it truly felt like Christmas.

Growing up, I was always relegated to the kitchen to help my mom prepare food. Call it deep-rooted sexism, or whatever else, but I was just as grateful to have to do work *inside* while Mom sent the boys *outside* to make sure the house was ready for guests. Even as adults, and even with no other guests coming, today was no different.

After Wendy and I got the turkey in the bag, we set it on the aluminum pan together.

"All right, I'm just about done with the pie and then I can add the seasonings to the turkey," Mom said. "Wendy, why don't you put those buns in the oven?"

Wendy started to comply as I washed my hands at the sink.

Mom snickered. "That's funny. Bun in the oven. Speaking of, when are you and Keith going to give me another grandbaby?"

I froze where I was. It wasn't until the water began to get too hot that I switched it off and then slowly turned to face my sister-in-law. I wondered how many comments like that Mom had made to her, especially yesterday when they were home alone together.

"Mom, are you done with that pie?" I jumped in to rescue. "I might as well clean up as we go so we're not spending another hour cleaning up the kitchen."

"Oh, yes. You can set the pie off to the side until it's ready to go in the oven."

Mom and I switched places so she could wash her hands and I could clean up the mess she had made while preparing the dessert. As I stepped up to the counter, I glanced over at Wendy, who gave me a friendly smile. I didn't know if Keith had told her that he had told me about their trouble to conceive, but Wendy looked grateful for the distraction regardless.

Chapter 23

It's funny how, even though I haven't been to a Mass in a couple years, things came back to you so naturally. I remembered to kneel when I was supposed to kneel, to sit when I was supposed to sit, and to shake hands at the right time. I remembered the steps of the Mass, as if I had been a weekly attendee, which, of course, I wasn't any longer.

I recognized many familiar faces in the crowd. Many people I had grown up with. Some I had been friends with, others not so much. But in a small town like Corfu, even if you weren't *friends* with someone, you knew an awful lot about them and their family that, even years later, I felt as though I knew them.

Usually that bothered me. Tonight, it didn't.

Once the Mass had ended, Mom very proudly showed me and my brothers off to her friends.

"Yes, my *whole* family is in town to spend Christmas with me," she told Cheryl Snipery, who had been the church busybody, from what my mother had told me through our many phone conversations. Tonight, however, my mother *wanted* word to spread that we were home for Christmas.

I indulged her and acted the part for the time being. Mom was happy, and I was glad that I was among the reasons for it, even if she did embellish on my life.

"Yes, she lives in *New York City*! And she's a *designer*!"

If only her friends knew how basic and simple and *boring* my life really was, they wouldn't be nearly as impressed with those bits of information. But these people were from Corfu, who had probably only ever seen New York in movies or the occasional trip there, so the whole place was still mystifying to them.

"Linda?" Amy Crittenden said from behind me. When I turned to face her, she smiled and leaned toward me for a hug. "I thought it was you! I never expected to see you here!"

I pulled away after the hug and nodded. "Yeah. I came home to visit Mom." I wondered if there would

be more visits home after the baby came—if I even decided to keep the baby. Was I going to hell for even considering that option in a church?

"Oh, how nice! And I see your brothers are here too. Are you all staying with your mom then?"

I nodded again, suddenly feeling three feet tall for the way that she worded it. "Mm-hmm."

"So sweet! I'm sure your mother loves that."

"She does. So what have you been up to?"

Amy Crittenden was not my favorite person in high school, but I was desperate to put her and her life in the spotlight and not me and mine.

"Oh, I got married, then divorced, and now I'm remarried."

"Well, um…congratulations?" I wasn't sure which part she'd take the compliment for, the failed marriage or the new one.

"Thanks," she said. "Never got around to having kids with all of that shuffling around, but—" She shrugged. "—what are you going to do?"

Was it selfish of me to be happy that she didn't have a perfect life either?

"Yeah, that's true. Well, I'm glad you're happy." I started to wind down the conversation. I was about to pull out the *It was nice seeing you* when she hit me with a bombshell.

"Are you married?"

I cleared my throat. "Um…no, I'm not." Then I pulled out the thing that seemed to be a way to indicate that I was *super* successful, even though there really was no credence to the assumption. "Actually, I live in New York City now."

"Oh really?" Amy asked, impressed.

"Yep, the Upper East Side. Rent's a little steep but—" I shrugged, mimicking Amy from a few moments ago. "—what are you going to do?"

"Right, right."

I looked past her and spotted Lyle Cleveland. The floor of my false bravado fell out from under me. How did he keep showing up whenever I left Mom's house?

"Well, it was nice seeing you," Amy said to me.

She gave me another quick hug, which I only half noticed, then moved toward the doors.

"Did I hear that right?" Lyle stepped toward me after Amy moved on.

"That depends…which part?" I didn't think there was anything I had said that was a lie. Maybe an embellishment, but no outright lie.

"You live in New York now?"

"Yeah. I work at a marketing firm as a graphic designer."

"Wow." He reared his head back a little, as if he was physically hit by my words. "That's impressive."

I shrugged. "Yeah, well…" I didn't find it that impressive. I had a creative eye, so designing came naturally to me. And with that skillset I found a job. But as the only girl in the family, I had been predisposed to diminish my capabilities.

"You want to know something funny?" he asked.

"Always," I said so naturally. It was like we were transported back in time to when we were teenagers. When we were dating. I scrambled my brain, trying to remember the reasons we broke up. I didn't remember ever hating him or being angry with him. Actually, whenever I looked back at that time of my life, it was always happy memories that came up. And if the way I felt through our last several interactions the last couple days, the butterflies still showed up in my belly whenever he was around.

"I live on the Upper *West* Side."

My eyes bugged out. "How did we never run into each other?"

He laughed. "Well, it kind of *is* a big city. But I work at Columbia University. I'm a history professor. I mostly stay around in that area. I don't really venture out much."

"Wow. A history professor. *That's* impressive."

Now he shrugged. "Meh. I like history and they needed someone to teach it."

I smiled. We both had the same approach to work.

"Actually, I'm considering making a change back to Western New York," he said.

"How come?"

"I feel like I'm outgrowing the city a little. It's fun, I like it, but it was never a long-range plan," he explained. "Besides, it's expensive, and I think the likelihood of me getting tenured there is slim. My thinking was, since I have experience working at an Ivy League college, I can kind of have my pick of any of the schools up here. Less work, only slightly less pay, and I think my chances of getting tenured are probably greater. Besides, my parents are getting older and my brother lives in Seattle, so I'm kind of the one who keeps an eye on them."

I smiled again. We had similar situations. Both of us were the oldest in our families, and both of us felt a commitment to our aging parents. "Well, it sounds like you have a plan."

"What about you? Have you ever thought about moving back?"

I paused as I considered it. I hadn't ever seriously thought about it before, but now that I had a baby coming—and that I'd actually acknowledged that fact—it was time that I made some plans for the future. Mom was selling her house, but did she have

to? I knew she didn't want to. But did I want to move back into the house that I grew up in? The place I was desperate to get away from?

But what would I do for work? Would my boss let me work remotely? Would that hinder me from future promotions? Did I care?

"Not until just this moment."

He smirked. "Well, you should think about it. I would love to catch up with you. After my wife and I split up, it's been kind of lonely on my own. I would love to reconnect with an old friend."

I bit my lip to try to hide my smile. It didn't work.

"Linda, let's go!" Marty called from behind Lyle. He didn't look happy. And beyond him, Luna looked just as frustrated.

I searched around to find the rest of my family and saw Keith shaking hands with one of his former friends. Mom and Gary were talking with an older woman I didn't recognize, along with Wendy, who was holding Connor. My family was funneling toward the exit.

"I guess I'm being summoned," I told Lyle. "I would love to catch up sometime. Maybe before I head back to New York? Or maybe when we're both in New York?"

"Yeah, I'd like that. Is your number still the same?"

"Same number from when I was sixteen," I said. "No sense in changing it."

"Great, then I still have it. I'll call you."

"Linda! Let's go!" Marty called impatiently.

"Bye," I said breathlessly as I forced myself to walk away from him.

Why had we ever broken up?

THURSDAY,
December 25th

Chapter 24

"Merry Christmas!" Mom cheered as I stepped into the kitchen first thing in the morning.

Everyone else was already up. Even, to my surprise, Marty and Luna. Although, both of them seemed to be looking everywhere *but* at each other. And Marty, especially, seemed exhausted.

"Merry Christmas," I mumbled.

Connor, who was oblivious to the celebrations, cheered along with my mother, which made everyone laugh.

I stepped into the kitchen and reached for the coffee pot, but thought better of it. I hadn't done any detailed research, but a part of my brain was warning me that too

much caffeine was bad for a pregnant lady. I must've read that somewhere.

I was still undetermined if I was going to embrace that title, but I decided to avoid the coffee to play it safe. Instead, I opted for tea, and I draped the teabag inside a mug and then set the mug under the Keurig for hot water.

"All right, everyone get dressed!" Mom said. "Santa came last night and—"

"Mom," Keith started, "we're all adults, we don't have to—"

Mom shot daggers at him, then gestured with her head toward Connor. "*Santa* came last night."

Keith let out a deep breath as he gave in to her act. He couldn't keep the smile from his face.

"Like I was saying, everyone needs to get dressed so we can open presents!" Mom cheered.

Gary cleared his throat. "Um, honey. I think you need to eat something first."

"No, I'm *fine*," she insisted.

He tilted his head down and glared at her.

"Okay. All right. We can eat first."

"How about a hearty, hot breakfast?" Gary suggested. "I'll cook—*and* do the dishes."

"Oh, Merry Christmas to me!" Mom said.

"Doesn't Gary normally do the dishes?" Marty asked.

He nodded.

Mom waved it off. "Well, that's beside the point. Gary is making a hot breakfast!"

"Bacon, eggs, and toast," Gary warned. "Nothing fancy."

"And nothing that'll take too long," Wendy said. "Which is good, because Connor has about twenty minutes before the demon cry starts and he demands food." 

Gary finished off his coffee, then got to his feet. "Then I'd better get started." 

I bounced my teabag in my cup and nodded to  the stairs. "And I'm going to take advantage of the break to go take a quick shower."

"Linda!" Mom said. "Join the family! It's  Christmas!"

"And I will," I assured her. "But I would like to be  clean before I partake in today's festivities. I'll be  quick. Promise."

Truth be told, I wasn't hungry in the slightest.  Mom's feast last night was more than filling. And the fact that we had another one lined up for tonight  made me not want to eat a thing.

And yet, the idea of bacon, eggs, and toast for  breakfast *did* sound good.

I carried my tea upstairs with me and set it on the  dresser. I turned to my bag to retrieve some clothes

when I heard a knock at the door. A few seconds later, Keith stepped in.

"Hey," he said. "Can I talk to you for a sec?"

"Way to wait for a response," I said. "What if I was naked?"

He looked me up and down. "But you're not."

I rolled my eyes. Even as adults, there were no boundaries with family, apparently.

"I really need to talk to you," he said.

I brought my eyebrows together, unsure of what could possibly be so urgent on Christmas morning. "Uh…sure. But I really do want to take a shower, so we're going to need to make this quick or Mom will—"

"This shouldn't take long," he said. "I just wanted to say that I heard about your…situation."

I was still confused until it registered with me where his hands were gesturing toward: my belly.

I was going to kill Marty.

"He wasn't supposed to say anything," I snapped.

"Well, I'm glad he did. Linda, this is huge. Why didn't you tell us?"

I shrugged. "We haven't talked in years. Now we're suddenly spending Christmas together and I'm going to unload one of my most personal secrets on you? Especially when I know that you and Wendy

are having a hard time having another baby? I mean, I wasn't even *trying* to get pregnant and here I am."

Keith shook his head. "This has nothing to do with me and Wendy. This has to do with you. I know we haven't come across as very supportive in the last few years—"

"We live entirely different lives, Keith," I reminded him. "We live on opposite ends of the state. We're just not close anymore."

"Maybe so, but I want to be. Again. Linda, you have my full support with whatever you decide. Marty said the same thing."

I sucked in a breath and crossed my arms. My youngest brother *had* told me that himself. "What about Wendy?"

"She…she might have a harder time with it," he admitted. "But it's not that she's not happy for you. She's just…working through her own issues. But she loves you too. And she wants to see you happy."

"Who says I'm not?"

"Marty said you seemed kind of scared about the whole idea."

"Well…yeah. I live far away from everyone. What do I know about raising a kid? Who will watch it when I'm at work? Or will I be one of those mothers who spends twenty-four hours with their baby and slowly goes insane and ends up on the evening news because she hurled herself off the fire escape?"

Keith raised his eyebrows, the hint of a smirk on his lips. "A little dramatic, don't you think?"

"I'm serious!"

"If you're worried about help, why don't you move back home?"

There was that suggestion again. Popping up everywhere.

I shook my head. "No. You saw Mom yesterday. She was so proud to say that I worked in *New York City*. I don't want to let her down."

"Take it from a parent, the only way you'd let her down is by not doing what makes you happy."

I decided not to remind him that his son was only a year old, and Keith didn't have experience with his kid going against his wishes. Still, it seemed like sound advice.

"What about the house?" I asked. "Mom might decide not to sell it if she thought I was going to move back in with her."

"Why don't you buy it from her?"

"Because I'm thirty-nine years old and I don't want to be going backward in life."

"Or maybe this would be going forward because you'd be taking over the house from Mom —*and* you'd be making her happy by raising a new

generation of the family in the house that she bought and paid for with her own money after she divorced Dad. You remember how much she used to work."

I let out a deep breath. I did remember. Better than Keith, probably. But was moving back home just to make her happy worth it? What did I want? I had to figure it out, and it wouldn't be decided right now.

"All I'm saying," Keith went on, "is that Mom has been a huge help with Connor, and we live over an hour away. And Wendy's parents, who live much closer, are irreplaceable. I think we'd lose our minds without the help of the grandparents."

"I don't know," I said dismissively. "Either way, nothing is getting decided today. It's Christmas and I don't want to think about this anymore." I knew I wouldn't be able to get it off my mind. "I need to take a shower, or Mom is going to flip that we're not following her carefully planned schedule of fun today."

Keith laughed. "That's true. But I want you to promise me one thing."

I huffed out a breath and eyed him. I was getting tired of him pushing the subject.

"You *at least* need to tell Mom," he said. "Before you go back to New York. She deserves to know."

There was no arguing with that. Mom was

supportive to a fault, even when she disapproved. "That's true. I'll tell her."

"Promise?"

"Promise."

He nodded. "Okay then." He started to turn to leave.

"Hey, Keith."

He spun around. "Yeah?"

"Thanks."

He smirked at me. "Anytime."

Chapter 25

By the time we all reconvened in the living room, Gary had already started a fire, Mom had picked the perfect music for opening gifts, and Wendy had poured us each hot chocolate to enjoy while we unwrapped our gifts.

In our family, each person opened one present at a time and we went around the room as if we were each taking turns in a board game. It took forever, but it was our tradition.

Mom re-explained the rules of Christmas:

"One gift at a time!"

"Make sure everyone sees what you've got!"

"We'll each take turns so that everyone gets a chance to open!"

I knew it was absurd to have "rules" for Christmas, but that was what I'd always known. After Mom went over the rules, Luna let out a frustrated sigh that everyone else just ignored.

Our fun would not be spoiled.

In years past, Wendy had even picked on us for our traditions, but since she and Keith had been married, she had gotten used to it. And now that we had a bigger group this year, I was looking forward to it myself. Going one-by-one helped spread out the Christmas cheer all day. We had spent a month or more preparing for this day, it was only right that we tried to stretch it as long as possible.

"Who's going first?" I asked.

"I think Mom should," Marty suggested.

She shook her head and waved off the idea, but the rest of us agreed with Marty with such force that Mom had no choice but to accept the gift that he handed her.

"That's from Keith and Wendy," Marty told her.

It was a small box. We normally grabbed the smallest boxes that we could see up front, again calling back to when we were kids and Mom would make us wait to open the biggest boxes for last. She was a bit sadistic when it came to Christmas and

D. ALLEN

wanted to ramp up the anticipation as much as she could.

Then again, with the way that she explained the rules this year and how we all so willingly followed along with them, maybe we were all a little sadistic too. Maybe there was some truth to Luna's grumbling.

Nah.

Mom carefully unwrapped the small gift, revealing a jewelry box beneath the wrapping. "Oh, you guys didn't have to spend so much money!"

"What makes you think we spent a lot?" Keith asked.

Wendy swatted his leg with her hand before quickly returning it to Connor's side, where she bounced him on her knee.

"What?" he asked. "She hasn't even opened it yet!"

"Yeah, open it, Mom!" I cheered.

Mom slowly cracked open the jewelry box and held her chest. "Oh wow. It's beautiful!"

"Do you like it?" Wendy asked.

"I love it!"

"Let's see it," Gary said, even though from his vantage point beside my mother, he could see it just fine.

Mom held it up, revealing a gold necklace that said "Grandma" at the base.

"Oh wow!" I said, knowing just how much it meant to my mother.

"We thought you'd like it," Wendy said. "We know how much you love Connor and even though we don't see each other as much as we'd like to, we want you to know we're always thinking about you."

Mom swatted away that comment and stood up to hug them both.

I couldn't help but think about the baby growing in my belly. The circumstances were entirely different. Would Mom be just as proud of this baby as she was of my nephew? I was suddenly terrified to tell Mom the truth, but Keith caught my eye and we exchanged a million words without speaking. I needed to tell her.

"Okay, who's next?" Gary asked after Mom took her seat again.

For the next two hours, we each took turns opening presents one-by-one. We knew there would come a day soon when Connor would not have the patience to wait, but that was okay. For now, we held our same traditions.

I couldn't help but wonder how the addition of my possible baby would complicate things. And would Barry want to be involved in the baby's life?

Would I need to juggle holidays with him, meaning that I'd potentially have to go through Christmas without seeing my baby? The baby was barely the size of a raspberry and yet I was already dreading the loss of him or her.

"Linda, it's your turn again," Mom told me, bringing me out of my thoughts.

I looked down and saw Keith handing me my next gift.

"This is from…" he glanced at the tag.

"Marty," I finished for him. I recognized the wrapping paper, and yet I somehow had missed seeing him wrap this particular gift. "When did you do this?"

He shrugged. "I have my secrets."

I tore into the wrapping paper, tossing it on the floor in front of me, and revealing a box. It felt pretty light, which had me confused. When I opened it, there was a note inside that simply read:

You're my sister and I love you. Never forget that.

It had been scribbled on a scrap piece of paper from Mom's junk drawer. It was something Mom ordinarily used to write her shopping lists on, a slip of paper meant to be thrown away after a trivial use, but this note was gold to me. I didn't know if it was

hormones or the moment, but this gift was suddenly the best one I had received all day, and I knew I'd hold onto it forever.

"What does it say?" Gary asked.

I folded it back up and clutched it to my chest. My eyes locked on Marty. I stood and crossed the room to hug him tight.

"Thank you," I murmured in his ear. "I love it. And I love you too."

Marty indulged me for a moment and then pushed me away. "Okay, okay. Enough with this sh—" He looked down at Mom and modified his sentence. "…show of emotion."

But as he took a seat, I could see him dabbing at his eyes.

"I think that's about it." Keith took the focus off of us. "Everything else has been opened."

"Are you sure?" Mom asked.

Wendy stood and looked under the tree. "Yup. That's everything." She rose up again and something caught her eye. "Hey, look at this!" She reached for an ornament and gently pulled it off the tree.

"Let's see." Mom walked up and stood beside her. "Oh, that's when the kids were little!"

"You couldn't get them to smile for a nice picture?" Wendy asked with a laugh.

"Are you kidding? They were so excited to open

presents that that was the best I could do."

"Let me see." I took the ornament from Wendy and studied it, feeling both Marty and Keith come up on either side of me to look over my shoulders.

Upon seeing it, I remembered the exact moment we took the picture. All three of us still in our pajamas, making goofy faces in front of the Christmas tree. It was still dark through the window, and I remembered waking up early, too excited to sleep any longer. That was probably my last year believing in Santa. Truth be told, I had probably stopped believing before the picture was taken, but among the magic of Christmas and trying to keep the secret alive for my brothers, I allowed myself to indulge in the fantasy for one more year.

All of it brought back a flood of other happy Christmas memories that was almost too overwhelming. Tears prickled my eyes again. Pregnancy hormones.

"That's hilarious," Keith said.

"We should recreate it!" Wendy cheered.

My brothers and I didn't immediately react to that declaration. Slowly, we turned to each other and made sour faces at one another. None of us liked the idea.

"Oh, that's a wonderful idea!" Mom said. "You should all change back into your pajamas and—"

"Mom," Keith protested, "we're not going to change into pajamas just for a—"

"Consider it another Christmas present to me," Mom said. "Come on! I wish they were matching pajamas, but any pajamas will do."

I let out a heavy sigh and saw just how excited Mom was about the idea. "Okay. Fine."

"No!" Marty groaned. "Linda, you can't cave!"

"It's just a picture," I said. "It's not going to kill us."

"But she's going to put it in next year's Christmas card!" he whined.

I shrugged and trudged up the stairs to change.

Twenty minutes later, my brothers and I were laughing and smiling as Mom and Wendy took a bunch of pictures of us. Gary held Connor and stood by with a smile. Luna, meanwhile, escaped into the kitchen to prepare a cup of tea.

But the three of us barely paid any attention to everyone else. Keith and Marty had the idea to get on all fours and have me climb on top of their backs, which resulted in lots of failed attempts and laughs that I was sure brought Kodak gold.

I may have been annoyed that Mom had invited my brothers to Christmas, but in the moment, as I was laughing harder than I had in years, I was grateful for the unexpected invitation.

Chapter 26

The rest of the day was fairly relaxing. We each indulged our new gifts. Keith put together one of Connor's new toy sets while Wendy dug through the drawers in the kitchen for batteries. Marty played with Connor, and Luna escaped upstairs, apparently deciding not to be part of the family on Christmas Day.

Mom, meanwhile, spent most of the afternoon preparing the sides for dinner. As if any of us were even remotely hungry.

By the time we sat down to eat, the energy from the morning had subsided. Everyone was more somber as we each took our seats.

Luna was clearly not happy with Marty, creating an

awkward tension between the two of them. Connor was starting to fuss more than usual after skipping both of his naps. Mom looked exhausted from preparing another feast for the second day in a row.

Christmas was work, and we all seemed secretly glad that the holiday was almost over. It had been fun, absolutely, but it was also exhausting.

We ate in relative quiet. My chest began to burn as I realized that this was my moment. Everyone was quiet and I had center stage to reveal my secret.

I took a break from eating my mashed potatoes, which I barely even tasted since I was so nervous. I cleared my throat. "I, uh, have something to say…"

Everyone picked their head up. I saw both my brothers look at me and give me slight nods of encouragement.

"Um…I'm…I'm pregnant."

Mom stared at me and blinked for a few seconds, then she leaned back in her chair and laughed. "Oh my, Linda! Here I was thinking that Marty and Luna would be the ones to give me more grandchildren before anyone else!"

Luna shot to her feet and threw her napkin on her plate. "I can't take this anymore! Martin and I are *not* together!"

Everyone at the table looked around at each other. I was so wrapped up in my nerves that I hadn't

D. ALLEN

even fully processed the message.

"You're not?" Mom's eyes widened in shock. More than they had when I had revealed my secret. "Then why did you come home with him for Christmas?"

"Yeah, that seems like a lot of work just for—" I started, but Luna cut me off.

"We went on *one* date until he learned what I do for a living," Luna explained. "Then he never called me back—until he needed something."

I leaned over to Marty. "Is she a prostitute?" I was glad that the attention was off me for a little bit.

He looked like he wanted to be swallowed up by the floor and disappear.

"An *escort*!" Luna shouted at me. "And Martin paid me to come home for Christmas and pretend like we're together. But all of this—" She gestured to us all sitting around the dining room table and made a face. "—it's all too much! You can't pay me enough money to pretend to be this sticky sweet. You're all disgusting!"

Mom barked out an insulted laugh, but didn't offer any other commentary, even though we all knew she had opinions.

Luna stormed upstairs.

I looked over at Marty. "Are you going to go after her?"

He shrugged and reached for his glass of wine. "Why bother? If she leaves, I don't have to pay her the rest of her money. And where's she going to go in Corfu? She'll be back."

"Wendy, honey, what's the matter?" Mom asked suddenly.

We all looked over and noticed for the first time that Wendy was crying. Keith had his arm around her.

"What's the matter?" Mom asked again.

Wendy waved it off and sniffled. "Sorry. I don't mean to be like this. I'm happy for you, Linda. I am. I promise. I'm just…I'll be fine. Really. I will."

Keith swallowed hard and turned to the rest of the family to explain. "Wendy and I have been trying for another baby for a long time and nothing's happened yet."

"I'm sorry, Wendy." I felt like such a jerk. I had *known* they were having issues — Wendy, especially — and yet I decided to blast my unexpected pregnancy to the whole family instead of telling Mom privately. "I didn't mean to —"

"Don't worry about it," Wendy said through more sniffles. "Children are a blessing. And you're apparently blessed while I'm…"

"Anything we can do to help?" Gary offered quickly before she could finish her thought. "I know

how hard it is to watch everyone else have kids when it just isn't happening for you. My first wife and I went through the same thing. The important part is to go through it together. We didn't, and that's one of the reasons we split up."

"I don't think that's—Mom, what's wrong?" Keith looked to the other end of the table.

Mom's eyes had gone wide. She sat back in her chair. Her face had gone pale and she clutched at her chest.

"Mom!" I shouted and shot to my feet to rush to her aid.

Mom didn't respond. She fell out of her chair and collapsed to the floor. Gary and I reached for her, but couldn't stop her body from hitting the hardwood. At least he caught her head. Whatever health issues she had been dealing with were coming to light now. It seemed we had all been keeping secrets.

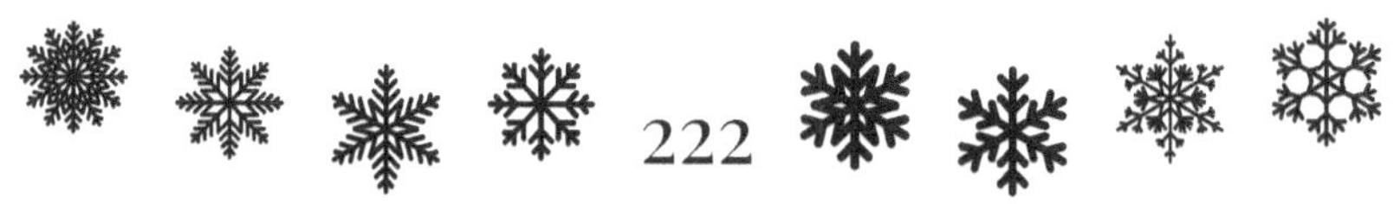

Chapter 27

Keith, Marty, and I all sat together in the waiting room at the hospital. Gary was in back with Mom. Luna had left, calling a rideshare back home—an expensive tab that Marty had said she'd be trying to charge him for. Wendy had stayed back home with Connor, who was getting ready for bed.

There had been an attempt at decorating the hospital for Christmas—red and green garland lined the top of the walls. Cutout prints of Santa and presents and other holiday scenes were taped up along the walls in an order that made sense to somebody. Despite all this, and the fact that it was *actually* Christmas Day, I didn't feel the least bit Christmassy at all.

The three of us all tried to get comfortable in the stiff chairs. It wasn't working. None of us were on our phones. None of us spoke. I knew for me, I couldn't stop replaying the last several days, weeks, and months in my head, trying to recount all of my interactions with my mother to pinpoint clues that I had missed that I should've picked up on. Clues that should've told me that she had been sick.

I had noticed that she had been napping a lot more than usual. She hadn't taken pictures as much as she used to. And the fact that she insisted we all come for Christmas and wouldn't tell us the others were coming was a sneaky change in behavior that she'd never done before. But there was no way I could've ever guessed that all of those clues would string together to wind us up in the hospital on Christmas Day. Maybe they still weren't related after all.

"I'm sorry," I said to my brothers, finally breaking our tense silence.

They both looked up.

"What?" Marty asked.

"I'm sorry," I repeated, looking directly at him. "It wasn't fair of me to judge you for having a relationship with our father."

"Look, Linda, I don't really want to get into this here—"

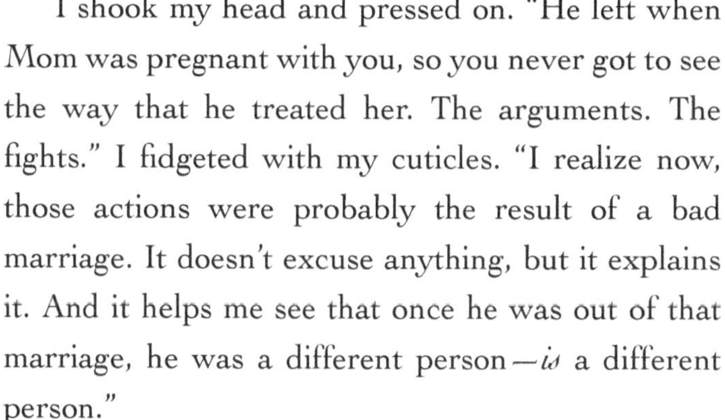

I shook my head and pressed on. "He left when Mom was pregnant with you, so you never got to see the way that he treated her. The arguments. The fights." I fidgeted with my cuticles. "I realize now, those actions were probably the result of a bad marriage. It doesn't excuse anything, but it explains it. And it helps me see that once he was out of that marriage, he was a different person—*is* a different person."

Keith watched the interaction carefully.

Marty looked confused. "Where is this coming from?"

I sucked in a deep breath and let it out slowly. "I'm saying this because I'm scared. I mean, we were just having Christmas dinner and now we're in the hospital, and Mom…" I couldn't finish as the sadness and fear overcame me.

In an instant, both of my brothers shot up from their seats and took the ones on either side of me, consoling me.

"Linda, don't worry about it," Marty said. "I think tonight's outbursts showed that none of us are perfect."

"I know, but if something were to happen, I wouldn't want you to think that I hate you," I sputtered. "Because I don't."

Keith reached over and handed me the box of

tissues that had been sitting on the short little table in the corner. I grabbed three in quick succession, then blew my nose and wiped at my eyes.

"I know you don't hate me," Marty said. "This past week showed that."

"And I'm sorry," Keith said, "if I ever made the two of you feel inadequate."

"Why would we feel like that?" Marty asked.

He really was oblivious sometimes. Then again, maybe I was the only one who got the impression that Mom thought Keith was perfect.

He shrugged. "For having a wife and a kid when you guys don't—"

Marty shook his head. "Don't ever *not* be proud of your family. We love them. And whatever you and Wendy are going through, you'll get through it. Together. With us."

"Thanks."

Then Marty turned to me. "And you be proud of your future child too."

I shifted in my seat, feeling suddenly uncomfortable with the attention from both of my brothers.

Keith took my hand and squeezed, leaning in until I looked him in the eyes. "Hey. We're going to help you take care of things. Marty and I both agreed on that."

I offered a tight smile. "That's nice to say, but the fact of the matter is that I live six hours away from here—and even farther from you, Keith."

"Why don't you just move in with Mom?" Marty asked.

"That's what I said!" Keith added.

"It'd be perfect!" Marty went on. "She's obviously sick, and I'm sure Gary could use a break from taking care of her."

"And adding in a baby to that mix will help?" I asked.

Before I had a chance to offer any other rebuttals, we saw Gary emerge from the doors leading to the wing of exam rooms. I was the first to jump up from my chair, and my brothers were quickly on my tail.

"How is she?" I asked.

"Yeah, is she awake?" Keith asked.

"What's wrong with her?" Marty added.

Gary put up his hands to stop the questions. "Why don't we all sit down?"

I nodded, even though my heart raced and my head spun. A million terrible scenarios ran through my mind.

After we retook our seats—the three of us across the aisle from Gary, as if he were going to read us a story—he took a deep breath and looked down, considering how to start.

"Well…your mother wanted to tell you herself," he started. "But she wanted to wait until after Christmas. Obviously, that's changed."

"What happened?" Marty asked. "Did she have a heart attack?"

Gary nodded. "Yes."

I gasped and sat back.

"Just a little one," he added quickly. "She's awake now, but very weak. She's been overdoing it these last few days and it's taken a toll on her heart."

"Was she diagnosed with a heart condition?" Keith asked.

Gary shook his head. "She has pancreatic cancer."

As Gary went on to explain that those with pancreatic cancer tend to be more susceptible to cardiac events, my mind spun, replaying my whole life in my head and every interaction I'd ever had with my mother. This felt like the end of the road, and I was completely blindsided by it. I was in no way ready to let go of my mother, and here I was faced with that reality.

"How long does she have?" Keith asked.

Gary's face soured as a heaviness overcame him. "The doctors…haven't given her a good prognosis."

At that, I burst into tears. This really was the end of my mother's life. Whether it was a week or a

year, the end was inevitable.

Keith put his arm around me and I leaned into him. It helped me feel less alone, although what I really wanted was for my mother to suddenly make a full recovery and live for another thirty years.

"Yeah, but she can fight it," Marty said. I heard the sadness in his voice too. The phlegm in his throat that said he was holding back more than he was letting on.

Gary just shook his head. I could tell that it pained him to deliver this news to us. And in that moment, I suddenly realized what I had been so resistant to see before: Gary loved Mom.

Of course, as her husband, I had always known that, but this was the first time that I realized the depth of that love and how it extended to us. We all might've been grown by the time he and Mom got married, but Gary didn't have any kids. I realized now that he saw *us* as his kids. In the absence of my relationship with my own father, I realized that Gary had been a father figure to me all along, which was a comforting thought in the wake of losing the only parent I'd ever had.

"Pancreatic cancer is one that very few people survive," Keith explained. "It's mostly undetectable until it's too late."

Marty refused to accept reality. He turned to

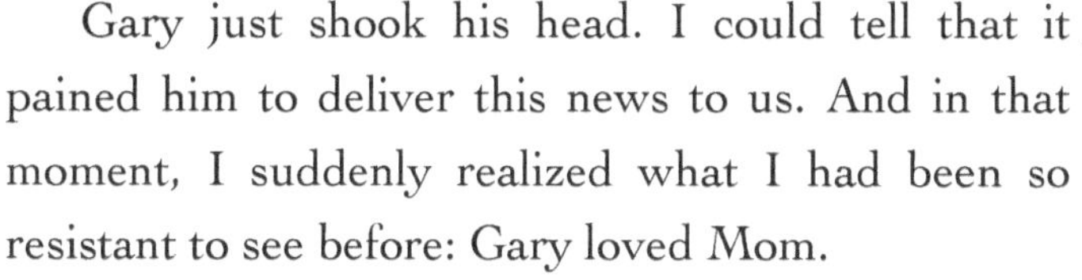

Gary. "When did she find out she had it?"

"Right around Thanksgiving was when the test results came back and confirmed it," he explained. "It was a few weeks before that when they noticed something on her routine scans."

Marty jumped to his feet. "*Thanksgiving*! And she didn't think to tell us that she's dying?"

I reached for his arm and pulled him back down to his seat.

After he was calm, Keith said, "I don't understand why she didn't tell us, either. It's been a month—over a month, really."

"She said she didn't want to worry you," Gary explained. "She said she wanted a family Christmas, especially seeing as it might be her last one."

I choked out another sob, and wiped at my eyes with my crumpled tissues.

"She *said* she didn't want to worry you kids," he went on. "I disagreed, but you're her kids and I wanted to respect her wishes. I wanted to keep her happy in her final months."

I took in a shuddering breath. "So how long does she have?"

Gary stared at the floor for a long while. If the conversation had been different, I would've thought he hadn't heard me. But he did. I knew that. He just didn't want to answer. Didn't want it to be real.

"The doctors said, if she's lucky…six months."

I sobbed again and turned into Keith, who wrapped his arms around me. I heard him sniffle.

"Can we see her?" he asked Gary.

"Yes. She's been asking about you."

Chapter 28

I was a sobbing mess when I went in to see my mother, where, despite the hospital gown and other hospital equipment hooked up to her, she looked perfectly healthy. She was looking at her phone and smiling at it. Maybe, somehow, Gary was wrong and Mom would live a long and healthy life.

I knew that was impossible.

My brothers and I surrounded her bed and Mom reached out with her hands to hold mine and Marty's, who stood closest to her. She smiled up at Keith.

"How are you feeling, Mom?" I asked, because I didn't know what else to say. I didn't want to barge into the room and demand an explanation for the deception.

I didn't want to spend what could be my mother's final moments yelling at her.

She shrugged a gave a smile meant to put me at ease. It didn't work. "Not too bad, considering…"

I sucked in a shuddering breath.

Mom looked at me with a guilty expression. "I suppose Gary told you what's been going on?"

"He kind of had to," Keith said.

"Yeah, I suppose so," she said solemnly.

"So…it's true?" Marty asked.

She nodded and squeezed his hand. "Unfortunately, it is, sweetheart. I'm sorry."

Marty's face contorted as reality hit him yet again.

"Why didn't you tell us?" I asked. It was not only a fish for an explanation, but also a lifeboat to Marty, who was on the brink of completely losing it and, I guessed, was desperate for a distraction.

Mom scoffed. "Oh, I didn't want to worry you."

Marty wiped at his eyes with his sleeve and sniffled. "Well, you're doing a great job of that." He chuckled, but Mom didn't find it funny.

Her face turned down. "I know. I should've told you when I found out. I never wanted to ruin your Christmas—or future Christmases with this terrible memory."

"We're not worried about that, Mom," Keith said.

"We're worried about *you*."

"And I appreciate that. But that's exactly why I didn't tell you kids," she explained. "Let's be honest, this is going to be my last Christmas."

"Mom!" I scolded.

She looked at me seriously. "It is, Linda. We can't live in a fantasy world. And I wanted to spend one last Christmas with all of my kids together in one house, just like it was when you were little. I wanted happy memories and reminisces, and, yes, even some sibling rivalry between you kids."  

I smirked through my tears. We had certainly delivered on that. 

"I didn't want the conversations to be about my cancer," Mom went on. "I didn't want the worry and the stress and the *sadness*. I wanted one last happy family holiday together."  

Marty wiped at his eyes again and snickered between sniffles. "We've been bickering so much, I wouldn't exactly call it *happy*."  

"No, but we were together," Mom said. "Besides, do you think you never bickered when you were kids? If anything, all of the sniping and yelling made it seem *more* like the happy Christmas memories I have of when you kids were little." She looked up at Keith. "Only now, we've added more people to our family, making it even better. I'm sorry you and  

Wendy are having such a hard time having another baby. When it's meant to happen, it'll happen. Just look at how far apart in age you and Marty are."

Keith took a seat at the edge of Mom's bed and placed a hand on her knee. He didn't say anything, and I wondered if that was so he could keep it together. Out of the three of us, he was the one who had so far remained stoic about all of this.

Mom looked up at Marty. "And I'm sorry that you thought you had to lie about your life in order for us to be happy—for *me* to be happy. You, yourself, are enough for me and, despite what they may say, your siblings as well. We're a family, and even though we disagree with each other, we love each other." She turned her attention to me. "And we're there for each other. Speaking of secrets, I wished you hadn't kept yours."

I looked down. "I know. And I'm sorry." I squeezed my eyes shut, trying to keep the tears in as a terrible thought occurred to me: Mom would never get to meet my child.

"Whether I'm alive or not, my dear, I will always be with you," Mom said, as if reading my thoughts. "Trust me, I never felt as close to your grandmother as I did when you were first born. I kept thinking about what my mother had done, or would do, and let that guide me as a parent. And—not to toot my

own horn, or anything—but I think I've done a good job raising you that I know you'll be thinking about me often throughout motherhood." She smirked. "I'm never going away."

I hoped that was true.

"How are you so calm about all of this?" Keith asked.

She took a deep breath. "I've had time to think about this a lot. I've come to terms with it. My death is happening much sooner than I thought it would, but there's a time and a reason for everything." She let go of our hands to reach for her phone. "This past week has helped me a lot." She pulled up the picture on her phone—the one of us goofing around in front of the Christmas tree, trying to recreate the old one. "You may all say otherwise, but this picture says enough for me. You love each other, and you had fun together this week, even if you were mad at me for not telling you that all of you were coming."

She studied the picture. "To me, this picture shows me my three adult kids are happy, carefree, joyful, and full of love. *This* is what I wanted for Christmas. And that's what you've given me. It's also how I want to remember the three of you—and how I want to be remembered."

"Mom, don't—" Keith started, but Mom cut him off.

"No, Keith. I'm dying. There's no sense in denying that. What I want is to *live* in my last few months, however long I may have. I want you three kids to help me see and experience as much as I can. I'm not talking about going to see the Eiffel Tower — I don't think my doctor would even allow a trip like that. What I want to see if *you*. All three of you. Together, as often as you can. And I want to know that you'll still look this carefree and happy with each other after I'm gone." She held up her phone with the picture.

I nodded. "I promise."

My brothers echoed a similar response, and the three of us all hugged.

ONE YEAR LATER
December 25th

Epilogue

"Merry Christmas!" Marty cheered as he stepped into the house.

Lyle shook Marty's hand, then took the bag from off his shoulder. "Here, let me take that."

"Thanks, man." Marty looked over at me and wrapped both arms around me tight.

Even though we'd just seen each other a couple weeks ago to see the Festival of Lights in Hamburg, it felt good having his arms around me.

"Where's the little guy?" he asked.

I nodded up the stairs. "He's napping. He should be up soon. Do you need any help getting everything out of the car?"

"No, I can run out and get it."

"Let me help," Lyle offered.

The crunch of snow turned all of our attention out the door. Keith and Wendy had pulled in and they smiled and waved through the windshield of their car.

"Merry Christmas!" Keith called when he stuck his head out the door.

I could hear Ryan crying upstairs. "I gotta go get the baby," I announced, then disappeared up the stairs.

When I got up there, Gary was already pulling Ryan from the crib. I paused in the doorway and watched as Grandpa Gary went to work, cooing and talking to my son as he changed his diaper after his nap.

Gary turned around with Ryan in his arms and startled when he saw me standing in the doorway. "Oh! I didn't see you there!"

I smiled at him. "Keith and Marty are here."

"Well then, you should go back and see Mom," he said to Ryan as he handed him off to me. "I'll go down and see if they need help."

"Lyle's already on it," I told him.

"More hands can't hurt."

Downstairs, the overnight bags lay by the door and Wendy was knelt beside the Christmas tree as

she laid out the gifts that they had brought. Connor stumbled around the living room while the guys sat on the couches—we had upgraded to two couches now that the house had become the centerpiece of the family holidays.

"Gary!" Marty cheered as he stood to give our step-father a hug. Keith followed suit, and I took a seat on the floor, leaning against the couch and wedged Ryan in the space between my legs so I could support him upright. He had been doing well sitting up on his own, but still needed a lot of support.

It was amazing how with the arrival of my brothers, the whole house had suddenly felt like Christmas. The tree was lit, the soft music still played, and the scent from the candle burning carried throughout the house. Best of all was my family, surrounding me again where they should be.

Gary clapped his hands together as he backed toward the kitchen. "All right, now it's officially Christmas vacation. Who wants eggnog?"

"I'll take some," Marty said.

"Yeah, I'll have some too," I said.

Keith looked over to Wendy and smirked.

"I'll take the non-alcoholic version if you have it," she said.

My eyes widened and I sat up straighter, which caused Ryan to stumble. I grabbed his arm just

before he crashed to the floor, and righted him. "Wait a minute," I said to my sister-in-law. "Are you…?"

Wendy couldn't contain her excitement and she smiled widely as she nodded. "Yes! I'm pregnant!"

I scooped up Ryan so I could jump to my feet and hug her. Marty and Gary joined me, and we roped Keith into the hug as well.

"Oh, I'm so happy!" When I had given birth to Ryan, I knew that Wendy was supporting me, but I could also tell that it had hurt her a little to see it happening for me but not for her. Still, she was immensely helpful these first few months of Ryan's life, especially since I no longer had my mother to rely on for questions.

"And we made sure she was through the first trimester, so hopefully there won't be any more complications," Keith added.

"That's awesome, guys," Marty said. "Congrats."

"Even more reason to celebrate." Gary left to get the eggnog.

Lyle took Ryan from my arms. He had been another integral part of my emotional survival this past year. After we had reconnected last Christmas, we had met back up in New York for a few dates that went well. That streak was interrupted when Mom ended up in the hospital around Valentine's Day, which prompted me to take an extended visit back

home. By the time I had arrived at Mom's bedside, we had enough time to say our final goodbyes before she passed away an hour later.

In the wake of my grief, Lyle had called me, unaware that my mother had passed, to tell me that he had watered my plants in my apartment. As if, at that moment, I cared about my plants at all. That small act of kindness made me feel even closer to him, but it was when he showed up at my mother's funeral that I knew that he was someone special.

After I told him I was pregnant, he had been incredibly supportive and non-judgmental. To the contrary, Barry, my ex, seemed most concerned about whether I was going to take him to court for child support. Since I had already talked to my office about moving back to Corfu and working remotely, I knew I didn't need Barry's income to support Ryan, so I told him that if he signed away his parental rights, I wouldn't come after him for child support. That way, it was a clean break for both of us. I still had Barry's contact information for Ryan if he ever decided to find his father, but that wouldn't be until much later.

In the meantime, Lyle had also relocated back to Western New York, and we resumed our relationship here where, after I had Ryan, he had basically been living with me and Gary in order to help take care of Ryan while I finished settling Mom's estate with my brothers and Gary.

The reminder of Mom, coupled with Wendy's pregnancy, brought tears to my eyes as I settled back into the couch.

"What's the matter, Lin?" Marty asked.

I shrugged. "Just thinking about Mom. She would've loved to hear this news."

We all sobered as that thought settled in everyone's minds. In two sentences, I had brought down the happy mood.

"She heard." Gary brought over a tray filled with several mugs of eggnog and set it on the coffee table in between the two couches. "And she's happy about it. In fact, she's smiling down at all of us right now, happy that we're together again. Happy that you're all keeping your promise of being together." He looked over at me. "Happy that you're doing so well as a single mother, especially that you've taken over this house. The idea of selling this place was something your mother was really struggling with."

"She was?" Keith asked. "Then why did she tell us she was selling?"

Gary shrugged. "What choice did she have? This house is too big for me alone, and she knew she wasn't going to be here much longer. Of course, we never foresaw any of you moving back in here. I

know she's happy that it's staying in the family now, just as she's happy that the family is growing." He smiled at Keith and Wendy. "The fact that the two of you persevered through a very difficult time in your marriage brings her so much pride."

The way Gary talked was like Mom was still here with us, and I loved that. I loved the idea of her still being a part of our lives, especially as these positive changes happened, thanks to her influence.

Gary turned to Marty. "And she's very proud of you, sir. She's always been most worried about you, but you're showing her that there's nothing to be worried about. And the fact that you're talking to a girl who likes you for you and not because you're paying her is a step in the right direction."

Marty put a finger to his lips to shush Gary, but it was too late. The cat was out of the bag.

"You are?" I asked. "When did this happen?"

"Yeah, we just saw you a couple weeks ago and you didn't mention anything," Keith added.

"It was *supposed to be* a secret." Marty glared at Gary with a smirk.

"Why didn't you invite her to Christmas?" I asked.

"It's still in the early days," he said. "Relax."

Gary winked at him. "Regardless, you're all making your mother proud. The fact that this house

continues to be filled with love and family is a legacy that she always wanted to leave behind. You should all be proud of yourselves for the changes that we've made as a family. And the fact that you now consider me part of the family…" He faltered as emotion filled him. When he spoke again, it was quieter, more scratchy. "It means the world to me."

Wendy rose and hugged him. "That was beautiful, Gary. You and I might be the outsiders of this group, but we're still just as much family as anyone else."

"That's good," Gary said with a smile. "My name's on the house now and without me, you wouldn't have a place to host the holidays anymore."

Everyone laughed. I loved that Mom's memory was not a difficult one. That whenever I thought of her, I didn't remember the hurt, but remembered the happy. The memories.

"So Marty," Keith said. "Tell us about this girl."

Third DATE

Third Date
FEBRUARY

The familiar noise of the city wrapped around me as I came up the steps from the subway to Union Square. The cold winter wind went right through me as I pressed on through the small park to head to work.

I avoided the slush from the snow that had been trampled down by other commuters, and enjoyed the momentary reprieve from having people on all sides of me in the confines of the sidewalk. Here in the park, people gave you space.

My phone rang and I was tempted not to take the call in the morning rush, but I saw that it was Keith and so I answered it and let the call go right to my wireless ear pods.

"Hey, Keith," I said cheerily. "What's up?"

I had been having regular conversations with both my brothers since Christmas, just like I had always been having with my mom.

"Hey, Lin." His voice was somber. A complete contrast to mine.

I stopped where I was as the tone in his voice struck me. "What's wrong?"

"Gary took Mom to the hospital last night," he said.

"What? Why didn't anyone call me?" The wind and the snow and the crowd of people rushing to work didn't matter anymore. It was as if they all had disappeared. I suddenly felt a million miles away from where I should be: home.

"He wasn't sure what it was until the doctors ran some tests," Keith explained. "Gary said he thinks this might be the end. How soon can you get home?"

My mind spun. I had to notify work, pack a bag, book a flight, get to the airport, then once I was in Buffalo, I had to somehow get to the hospital—I didn't even know which one she was at yet.

"Um…as soon as I can," I told him. "I'll keep you posted."

"Okay. Hurry home, Lin. Love you."

"Love you too."

I spun around in the opposite direction I had

been rushing in just moments before. I swiped through my phone and pulled up my boss's number.

The words, "My mom is in the hospital" rushed out of me with no feeling at all. I was in crisis management mode, and all emotion was pushed aside.

It wasn't until I was waiting at my gate at LaGuardia Airport that the realization that I may be about to lose my mother sunk in. All of a sudden, my chest began feeling tight, I was short of breath, and tears prickled my eyes.

I was about to lose it right there in the airport, in front of a bunch of strangers.

My phone buzzed, pulling me away from my grief for a moment. It was a text from Lyle. We had gone on two dates so far and had plans for a third…tomorrow night.

Shoot.

HOW DO YOU FEEL ABOUT MATINEES? WOULD YOU WANT TO SEE A SHOW AND THEN GO TO DINNER AFTERWARDS?

I began to type out a response, but he sent another text before I could finish.

JUST A REMINDER, EVEN THOUGH WE WILL BE GOING OUT ON VALENTINE'S DAY, THIS IS **NOT** A VALENTINE'S DAY DATE. THIRD DATES AREN'T REALLY THE PLACE TO FULLY EMBRACE THE VALENTINE'S DAY SPIRIT...

I smiled. During our last date, when we had made plans for the third date, I had pointed out that we would, in fact, be spending Valentine's Day together. We both agreed that we would treat it as a sort of "anti" Valentine's Day date and we'd save our "real" first Valentine's Day for next year, pending the state of our relationship by then.

I typed out a response:

SORRY! I HAVE TO CANCEL. I'M ACTUALLY AT THE AIRPORT NOW. MY MOM IS IN THE HOSPITAL.

NO NEED TO BE SORRY! I HOPE EVERYTHING IS OKAY.

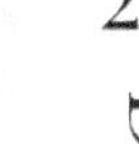

I DON'T THINK IT WILL BE, BUT THANKS.

I closed my phone and sat back. This was going to be a hard day and I wasn't sure I was prepared for it. I knew that when I got back home and saw my brothers and Gary that I'd feel better. Comforted. Supported. Even if I still felt like my world was crumbling apart.

My phone buzzed with another text from Lyle.

EVERYTHING WILL BE OKAY. IT'LL JUST TAKE TIME. TEXT OR CALL ME IF YOU WANT TO TALK.

The look on my family's faces was hard to see when I stepped into the hospital room. And then I took a step further and saw my mother laying in the hospital bed, attached to wires and monitors that slowly beeped softly, indicating her continued life, and I knew I would've taken the mournful look on my brothers' and Gary's faces over the sight of my mother at the end of her life.

And I knew this was the end, even if I didn't want to face it.

"Mom," I gasped out as I rushed to her side.

She raised her arms weakly as I walked up to her and pressed her frail body against mine. All I felt were the bones beneath her skin, and suddenly all I could think of was how strong she used to be back when she was able to cook us dinner with a toddler Marty propped on her hip.

"How are you feeling?" I asked, not sure of what else to say.

"I've been better." Her eyes were glassy, like it took a lot of strength just to keep them open. "I'm glad you came."

I squeezed her hand as I blinked away the tears. "Wouldn't miss it."

Keith walked up to me and rubbed my back. I slipped my free hand around him and leaned my head against his shoulder.

"Thanks for calling me," I said.

"I'm surprised you got here so fast."

I smiled a humorless smile. "It's a good thing I moved to the largest city in the country. Most travel options were available to me."

"Did you fly?" Mom asked from the bed. Her voice was so soft I almost didn't hear it over the hum of the monitors. I wondered how much pain she was in. Or rather, how much medication she was on to combat that pain.

"Yeah. It was only about an hour-long flight. I took a taxi here from the airport."

"That must've…" Mom's voice trailed off, but she raised her hands and rubbed her thumb over her fingers. I put together the rest of her sentence in my head: *That must've cost you a lot.*

I shrugged. "It doesn't matter how much it cost, Mom. I wouldn't miss being here with you."

Mom didn't reply. Her eyes were closed and the soft rise and fall of her chest told us that she had fallen asleep.

I let out a sigh—a heavy breath I didn't realize that I'd been holding since Keith had first called me that morning—and settled into the chair beneath the window.

Marty took the seat beside me and held my hand while Keith leaned against the windowsill next to my chair.

Gary walked up with his arms crossed and his face deep in thought.

"So…how is she?" I asked. "Really?"

"It's liver failure, which is common with patients with pancreatic cancer," he said. "The doctors say that some of her other organs will probably start failing as well."

"So…this is it, then?" It wasn't really a question, and I didn't expect anyone to answer me.

Keith put his hand on my shoulder and Marty squeezed my hand tighter. I had no idea what I would do without my mother in my life, but I was glad that I still had my brothers and Gary.

"Linda." I woke to Marty shaking me.

I opened my eyes and made out his shadow in the darkness. The sun still hadn't come up and I felt exhausted.

"What's the matter?" I sat up straighter and took stock of the room after being jolted awake — I had to get used to this kind of wake-up when the baby came.

"Gary got a call from the hospital. Mom's crashing. We gotta go."

My feet were on the floor before he even finished talking. I crossed the room to the dresser, where I had set my bag, and dug for a pair of socks. I didn't care how I looked. We needed to get to the hospital.

Marty had the same idea, since he was wearing shorts and a plain white T-shirt. Even though it was twenty degrees outside, neither of us would notice.

"Did you call Keith?" I asked as we raced down the stairs.

"Gary was calling him."

"Ready?" Gary was already at the door when we

came down the stairs. Coat on, keys in hand.

"No," I said honestly. "But here we go."

By the time we got to the hospital, we met Keith in the lobby and went up to the floor where Mom had been admitted. Her doctor met us in the waiting room on her floor. He had a sad expression on his face and he quickly ushered us down the hall into a grief room.

I knew what it meant, but it wasn't until we were all in the private room and he had delivered the news that she had passed that I finally broke down. Marty and I leaned on each other as we cried. Keith and Gary asked questions and thanked the doctor, even as they both shoved away their emotion.

I didn't listen to the specifics of what the doctor had said happened. The only thing that mattered was that Mom was gone. And I would be forever changed.

Was it morbid to start discussing funeral arrangements the same day someone died? I had no idea because, even as I approached my fortieth birthday, I was lucky that I had never lost anyone especially close to me.

Until now.

Gary, Keith, Marty, and I all sat around the dining room table at my mother's house — or rather, it was only Gary's house now. Wendy had brought Connor over and was keeping him occupied in the living room. Every once in a while, as the arrangements were being made, if things got too much for one of us, we would go join Connor and Wendy on the floor for some baby therapy.

"When your mother was first diagnosed, she had tried to put together a list of things to make this easier for you kids," he said. "None of it is binding or official, but this list was made by her."

I pulled the yellow notepad toward me and glanced at it. There were random thoughts jotted out everywhere and I had no idea how to follow her train of thought. Gary, however, seemed to know how to read the list. He tapped his pen along each note that was relevant.

"I wanted to run this by you kids before anything was finalized," he said. "She was, after all, your mother and you should all be as involved as you want to be."

"Thank you," Keith said.

Gary began running through the list: cremation, but with calling hours, donations to the library in lieu of flowers, slideshow of pictures *in addition* to photo albums available at the wake. Even hypotheticals

were laid out: "If none of the kids want the house, my urn should stay with my husband, unless one of the kids want to take it. If they argue over it, then set them up on a four-month period: Linda, January-April; Keith, May-August; Marty, September-December."

My head was spinning as we finalized plans and made changes based on the circumstances. I was grateful when my phone buzzed with a text and I excused myself to the next room to answer it.

It was from Lyle. It was a picture of a plant. Upon further inspection, I saw that it was *my* plant. In *my* apartment. I hadn't given him a key or anything.

THOUGHT YOUR PLANTS MIGHT BE THIRSTY, SO I BROKE IN AND WATERED THEM.

I smiled and tears prickled my eyes for an entirely different reason—although, I was hormonal from the pregnancy and rattled from the day's events. It wasn't that I cared about my plants—I often forgot to water them myself—but that small act of kindness in the wake of all this sadness made me feel incredibly grateful to have Lyle in my life.

Instead of replying to his text, I escaped upstairs

and called him instead.

"Lyle Cleveland's watering service, how may I direct your call?" he said when he picked up.

"How did you get into my apartment?"

"We specialize in finding plants in need and helping them in whatever way we can."

I laughed, which felt good. "I'm serious."

"I told the super I was your boyfriend and I was moving in and that I needed a key."

"And he just gave you one without being on the lease?"

"Scary, isn't it?"

I narrowed my eyes. "You gave him money, didn't you?"

"Yeah. And he made me promise to give the key back."

"How much?"

"A good magician does not reveal his secrets."

I rolled my eyes. "I want to know how much it costs to break into my apartment."

"More than you would think."

I smiled again. Lyle was willing to pay the super enough money just to get temporary access to my apartment, only to water my plants. Who was this man?

"Well, thank you," I told him. "I appreciate it."

"No big deal. How's your mom?"

I swallowed the lump in my throat.

"That bad, huh?" he asked in my silence.

"She passed away early this morning," I told him. "When we came home to get some sleep."

I heard him let out a heavy breath. "I'm sorry, Linda. That's…well, you know. I'm always here to talk if you need a distraction. Or want to talk about it."

"Thank you," I said. "My brothers have been great, but I may take you up on that offer."

"Anytime."

My cheeks hurt from smiling so much. I knew I was allowed to feel whatever I wanted at my mother's wake, but at the moment I was feeling more tired than sad. Of course I missed Mom and wished she were still with us, but with all the commotion of planning for the funeral and making arrangements to work from home for a while, reality hadn't sunk in yet.

As people moved through the line, hugging me and my brothers and Gary, I found myself reconnecting with old friends, smiling politely at acquaintances, and hugging complete strangers who had been close to my mother at some point in her life.

It had been a long day.

I considered dipping out for a few minutes to get something to drink and stop at the bathroom, but I feared that I'd run into someone in the hall and wouldn't get a chance to get back to the line.

And then my world rocked when I saw a familiar face step up and offer Marty a handshake and a quick "bro hug," before doing the same to Keith, who stood just to my left.

"You came?" I asked.

Lyle smiled. "Wouldn't miss it." He leaned down and gave me a hug.

I found myself melting into him, holding onto him for longer than I had with any of the others who had passed through the line. I felt my stress melt away as, for only a moment, I was safe and I could take off the mask I had been wearing.

When we finally parted, I blinked away the tears that had formed in my eyes and gave him a genuine smile, even though it hurt my face.

"I needed that."

"I could tell," he said. "Do you want me to stand with you?"

My heart ached with how sweet he was. Lyle truly was someone special. Why had we broken up as teenagers? Then again, both of us were different people back then.

"The crowd seems to be thinning out," Gary said from my right. "If you kids want to take a break, nobody will think any less of you. Your mother knows you were here."

Marty sank into the chair against the wall, just behind a large bouquet of flowers. "My feet are killing me."

"Mine too," Keith said.

Wendy walked up with Connor stumbling by her side, his hand stretched up to hold hers. "Everyone is loving the photo collages."

"Thanks for helping with them," Gary said. "How's it looking outside? Still cars?"

"Hard to tell," she said, "since they have to park across the street. But yeah, I think it's slowing down."

Keith looked at his watch. "Well, it's almost seven, so the calling hours are almost over."

Lyle looked down at me. "Do you want to get something to eat? Maybe take a break from all of this."

"Yes, please." I glanced back at my family. We'd all been staying at Mom's house together since she passed. It was nice, but I needed a break from all of the heaviness. "Don't wait up."

I expected some kind of commentary from Marty, but there was none. He must've been too tired to pick

up on it. The week had left us all emotionally fried and exhausted.

I took Lyle's hand and led him out into the cold. He had parked on the street a little ways down. I slid into the passenger seat and was greeted with plastic bags filled with newspapers and magazines tucked on the floor of the car.

"Sorry about that," he said when he got in. He reached over and tried to help move them out of the way for me. "I obviously don't have a car, so this is my mother's."

"Why does she have so many newspapers?"

He tossed his hands up. "Who knows? Maybe she knows someone who needs them. Maybe she has been meaning to recycle them. I try not to ask too many questions."

I laughed as he pulled onto the street and drove out of town. He took us into Batavia, since the few eating establishments in Corfu had already closed for the day.

It felt a little like we were teenagers again, joyriding in his mother's car to get something to eat just because we could. And it was exactly what I needed. A moment to be free. Free of responsibility. Free of emotion. Free of my life.

We settled on a small diner on the outskirts of Batavia. It used to be mine and my friends' late-night

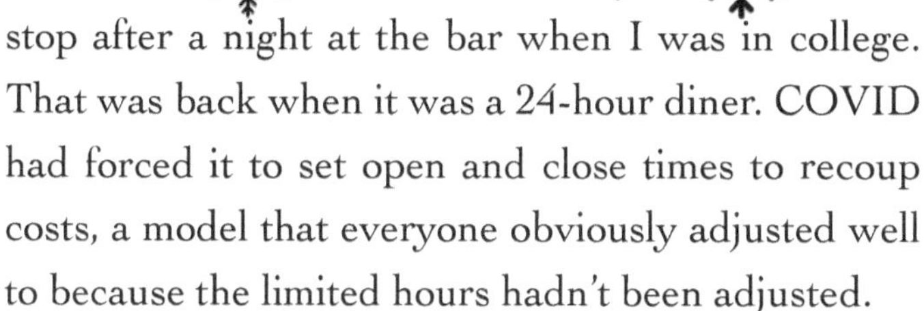

stop after a night at the bar when I was in college. That was back when it was a 24-hour diner. COVID had forced it to set open and close times to recoup costs, a model that everyone obviously adjusted well to because the limited hours hadn't been adjusted.

After the waitress came and took our orders—breakfast foods for the both of us, even though it was nearly eight o'clock at night—Lyle and I looked at each other across the table.

"Thank you so much for coming," I told him. "It really does mean a lot to me."

"I told you. I wouldn't miss it. I care a lot about you."

I smirked. My face didn't feel as sore as it had earlier. I was glad that Lyle was here. And I cared a lot about him too. But there were things he needed to know. Helping me through losing my mom was only going to be the start of the discomfort if things between us went anywhere.

"Are we counting this as our third date?"

He shrugged. "I don't know. This is a far cry from the plans I had for our third date, but if you want to consider it our third date, then sure."

"Let's see…you flew across the state to come to my mother's wake and kidnapped me to help me escape from all the grief from this past week. We've ordered food, we're both dressed up, and we have an

endless amount of time to be with each other…yeah, I think this could count as our third date."

He smiled. "Okay. Third date it is, then."

"And so *if* this is our third date, then that means our relationship must be progressing, right?"

Lyle scrunched his eyebrows in confusion. "Right…"

"And if our relationship is progressing, then there's something you need to know…I'm pregnant."

"Oh…" His eyebrows went up in surprise, but otherwise he showed no other emotion.

"Yeah…and I just started my second trimester, so I'm keeping it."

He nodded slowly. "Okay."

"So…yeah." I looked away, not sure of what else to say. He was being oddly quiet. Then again, I did kind of spring this on him.

"Who is the father?" he asked.

"My ex-boyfriend."

"Does he know?"

I nodded. "Yep. He's made it clear that he doesn't want to have anything to do with the baby. Or me."

"I'm sorry," he said. "So what's your plan? Or don't you have one yet?"

I took in a deep breath. "Um…well, I'm due in July. I've been toying with the idea of moving back here, but I'm not sure. It would be cheaper than rent

in New York, and after this week it's clear that my job will let me work from anywhere, as long as I'm doing my work."

"So what's stopping you? Do you *want* to live in New York?"

"Yes and no. I mean, yes, I love that I live there and I have that experience, but I'm also kind of over it a little bit, you know? Like, I've reached that goal, let's move on, you know?"

He nodded. "I do know. I'm making the same move, myself."

"You are?"

"It's something I was planning on telling you during our third date."

I smiled. "I thought we agreed this *is* our third date?"

"We did, but right now we're talking about you. So…are you going to move back to Corfu?"

"I don't know. I know my mom would've loved to have me take over the house—and it's a perfect house, and I love it, it just seems…I don't know. Do you think I'm moving backward in life?"

"Not at all. You'd actually be making a smart decision. Honoring your mother's life, relying on family and friends to help you navigate single motherhood. And since your job will let you work remotely, you'd be making a New York City salary with a Corfu cost of living. Could you imagine how much more you could give your child without the limitations of just trying to pay the bills?"

He had a point. I made good money at work, but there were definitely a lot of times where the rent had gone up and had necessitated some lifestyle changes, or some months where I had to watch my spending more closely. Living in Corfu would mitigate that.

"And I'm sure Gary would love the company."

"Oh yeah. I didn't think about him," I said. I didn't know how I felt about potentially living with Gary. We had grown closer since Christmas, but we still weren't *close*.

"He'll certainly help you with the baby," Lyle said. "And so will I, when I can."

I shook my head. "I didn't tell you about the baby to guilt you into helping me. That wasn't my intention."

"I know. I'm offering." He reached across the table for my hand. "I know you're probably scared. And I know it'll be difficult and awkward at times, but I like you, Linda. All of you. I want you in my life. Again."

The waitress came back with our food and set a big Belgian waffle in front of Lyle and a stack of pancakes in front of me. Then she set the sides of eggs, bacon, and toast all around us.

Heaven.

After she left, Lyle and I both quietly dug into our food. I couldn't help but notice how *normal* it all felt. Being with Lyle. The comfortable silence. My mother's passing had, for the first time all week, slipped my mind for a moment.

Even though she was one of my best friends and someone I would miss terribly, I also knew she wasn't really gone. If I did end up moving back to Corfu—and I had a feeling I was going to—then she would continue to be in my life. Every time I came home. Every time I stepped into a room and caught a memory of her: the way she had decorated it, her scent, the way she had organized the pantry. It would all remind me that she was still very much a part of my life.

Best of all, though, I had reconnected with Lyle, someone who wanted to help me maintain those connections with my mother and help me forge my own path forward.

As much as I was worried that I would be alone after my mother's passing, I knew that wasn't the case anymore. I wasn't alone. And while I was a far cry from feeling "okay," I knew that I would be. Someday.

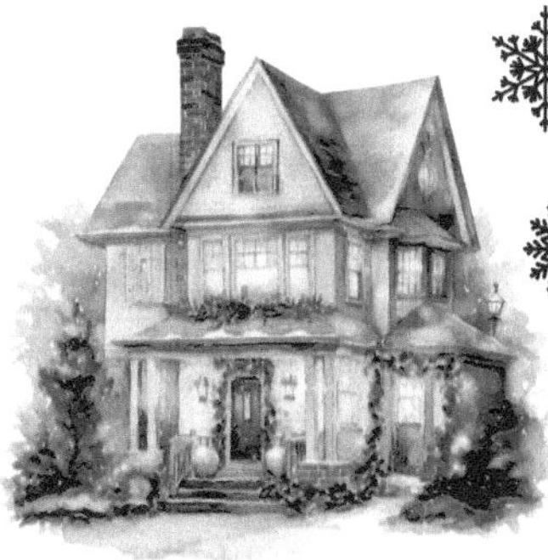

The idea for this book has been bouncing around in my head for years. I was inspired to write this book after listening to the song "Just For Now" by Kelly Clarkson from her first Christmas album, *Wrapped in Red*. The song details the chaotic nature of the holidays and how it's not always "merry and bright." I wanted to tell that part of the story, and I began to put together a loose plot that was Jonathan Tropper's *This Is Where I Leave You* meets *National Lampoon's Christmas Vacation*.

I didn't have a firm grasp of what I wanted the book to be, though, so it just kept getting put on the back burner in exchange for other books with actual plots.

Every Christmas, though, the ideas for this book would churn up again and I would promise myself that "next year" I would write it.

Then, after the success of my book, *Thanksgiving Day Parade*, I decided to devote more time to standalone books and writing books that I was excited to write. So I sat down and decided to put my ideas on paper to try to figure out where exactly this book was, and what it was going to look like.

And I made mistakes. As I was writing the first draft, the first 10-15 chapters were written in third person, omnipresent narrator voice, and it just wasn't working. I wanted to center the story from the perspective of one of the siblings (similar to what Jonathan Tropper did in his book that inspired this one), so I suddenly made the shift to first person, which necessitated cutting some chapters, but alluding to those scenes that had been cut as told to Linda by her brothers.

The story just worked better in the first person voice, and the writing became easy once I figured that piece out. The end result is a book that I'm very massively proud of because it fully did encapsulate that feeling of chaos and stress during the holidays. I also love that the central point of conflict is between siblings, which was fun to write, and didn't focus on a romantic relationship. Even Linda and Lyle's

relationship ended up being an afterthought and was amended in the editing phase to make it flow naturally. We need more stories that focus on different types of love and relationships, especially Christmas books that aren't just about romantic relationships.

I hope you've enjoyed the book! If you have, please leave a review online and tell all your friends about it! Thanks for reading!

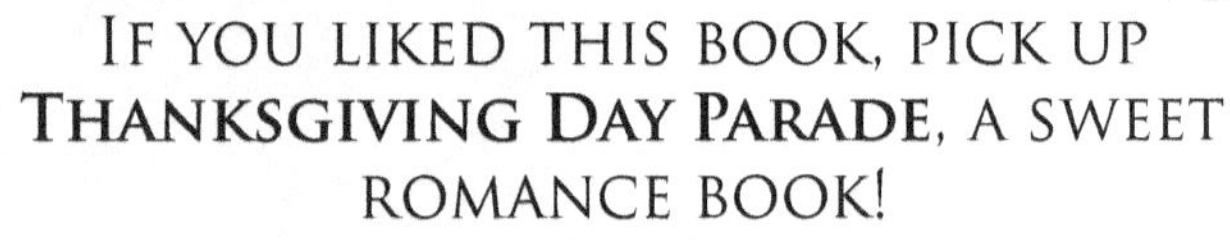

If you liked this book, pick up **Thanksgiving Day Parade**, a sweet romance book!

DavidNethBooks.com/d-allen-standalones

Julie Griffiths has had a crush on one of her friends at her hometown bar forever, but he's oblivious to her feelings. So when he and the rest of Julie's friends dare her to sneak into the Thanksgiving Day Parade in New York City, she accepts in order to impress her crush. Hours later, she finds herself on a crowded bus, equipped with nothing more than determination.

Brian Moore was already planning on going home to New York City for Thanksgiving, but a sudden breakup with his girlfriend gives him another reason. Heartbroken and lost, Brian isn't too happy when a woman sits beside him on the bus ride back to the city. Especially when she starts talking about her crazy idea to get into the Thanksgiving Day Parade.

Wanting to avoid an awkward encounter with his family, Brian agrees to help Julie accomplish her goal after it becomes painfully obvious that she has no plan for achieving it. But as the two begin to spend more time together, Julie starts to question her feelings for her friends back home while Brian realizes that maybe Julie is who he has been waiting for all along.

Thanksgiving Day PARADE

D. Allen

Chapter One
Thanksgiving Eve
Julie

Some people spend the night before Thanksgiving putting together everything they'd need to prepare the big feast the following day. Others sit back and enjoy a night off. Perhaps some frantically clean their houses for the arrival of extended family, or maybe run to the grocery store to see if they can find any more canned cranberry sauce.

Me? I avoided all of that. As much as I could.

"I'll take my usual," I told the bartender at my favorite local hangout on South Pearl Street.

Jim popped the top off a bottle of beer and set it on the bar. "Want me to start a tab, Jules?"

I passed him my debit card and nodded. "Of course!"

My plan was to stay out as long as I could to avoid the inevitable bickering between my mother and stepfather. It happened every night.

If it wasn't for the fact that she needed his salary to pay the mortgage and he needed her health insurance, I could pretty much guarantee the marriage would've crumbled a long time ago. Instead, they were trapped in this prison sentence, brought on by bureaucracy.

I've never been one for family time. We've never really been *tradition* people. Turkey and stuffing and going around the table to say how much we're thankful for wasn't really our thing.

The traditions I *did* enjoy, though? Spending time with people who are happy to see me. And after I snapped a quick picture of my beer bottle with the bar lights in the background, I grabbed it and stepped around the corner into the bowling alley, where three of my friends were just starting a game.

"Hey, cut me in!" I waved to my friends as I kicked off my shoes behind the bench and came around to greet them.

Brittany and Chloe both gave me hugs when they saw me. Eric was lined up like Fred Flintstone, all twinkle-toed and ready to hurl the ball down the lane. He did, and with a crash of pins, he tossed his hands up and roared, drawing all attention to him.

The lift of his shirt was hard to miss. He wasn't some muscle-chiseled model. His gut certainly showed that he liked beer. But his rugged handsomeness and overall charm made up for not having the perfect body. And that made my mind wonder about what the rest of his body looked like even more.

When he saw me, he cried out, "Julie!" and then wrapped his arm around me.

I put my arm around his bulk and leaned into him. His red beard tickled my face and some of my long blonde hair got tangled in it. I absently stroked my hair back into place when we parted, much sooner than I would've liked.

"You're late!" he said. "I've already got a strike on you!"

"We can add her in," Chloe said. "Each of us has only bowled once. Julie, if you want to play, it's your turn."

I nodded, then grabbed one of the balls in the return corral and stepped up to take my turn.

The marbled blue ball sailed down the lane and knocked out six pins. Not my best, but not my worst. I certainly needed warming up. My friends and I had tossed around the idea of joining a bowling league, but with me and Chloe being off to college and Brittany picking up as much overtime as she could manage, that really only left Eric and a few of our other drinking buddies, Tony and Otto. So, in a sense, the bowling league would have been a drinking league, making Eric and the other guys even more regulars of the bar than they already were.

"You're supposed to knock the pins down, Jules!" Eric cupped his hands around his mouth and shouted, as if he wasn't standing less than ten feet away from me. The hoarseness in his voice told me that he'd been shouting for a while. Clearly, he was already teetering on drunk. Factoring in his size and how often he drank, he must've started drinking at noon.

I tossed the ball down the lane a second time and knocked down two more pins. A total of eight. That was going to leave a mark on my score, compared to Eric's first-frame strike.

Chloe clapped her hands. "Good try, Jules!"

I retrieved my beer from the table, then found the picture I had taken of it on the bar and posted it to my Story. Then I snapped a picture of Brittany, who had stepped up to take her turn to bowl and posted that as well. Then, I leaned into Chloe and we both made kissing faces at the screen.

"Cute!" Chloe declared.

Another few presses on my screen, and that

picture was posted as well.

"Enough with the pictures, girls!" Eric said, with a fresh bottle of beer in his hand. "Jesus, this isn't a photoshoot."

I held up my phone and snapped one of him. He swiped at my phone and missed, resulting in a blurry picture of him. It looked artsy. I liked it.

"Sure, it is," I said. "Every day is a photo shoot!"

He tried again to take the phone from me, but I pulled it away in time, so he grabbed my wrist and spun me around so my back was pressed up against him. I giggled as we struggled, eventually sinking to the floor.

My heart fluttered with how close we were. There had been a lot more physical touches from Eric over the last couple months. I couldn't figure out whether he was flirting or not. Of course I wanted to *believe* that he was flirting, but my brain was telling me to put that wall up and not expect too much for fear of getting hurt.

"Looks like you're getting empty," Eric said.

My bottle was only halfway gone, but I recognized that it was an excuse to extract himself from the situation and avoid any further awkwardness.

Eric didn't do awkward.

In his absence, the game settled a bit. I took a seat next to Brittany while Chloe bowled.

"Are you dreading tomorrow as much as I am?" Brittany asked.

She had a perfectly normal family. A mom and a dad, two brothers, and even a family dog. But Brittany hated tradition and anything that made her feel normal. She felt trapped when she felt normal. Besides that, it was a forced day off from work for her, and when she was paid hourly, it mattered. She had wanted to go into work and get the holiday pay, but her mother had thrown a fit, so Brittany had no choice but to attend her traditional family Thanksgiving dinner, now laced with resentment between mother and daughter.

It wasn't quite the same situation as me, but it was still nice to commiserate with someone.

"Mm-hmm," I murmured. "Between my stepdad shouting at the stupid football game, my mother swearing and banging things around in the kitchen, and my brother being completely complacent to our messed up family, I would much rather skip the holiday."

"Right?" Brittany responded. "At least with Christmas we get gifts."

"*Then* there's a distraction," I said in agreement.

Chloe came back from the lane. "Where's Eric? He's up."

I nodded toward the bar. "Getting some refills. He'll be back."

"Again?" Chloe asked. "He just got another drink!"

Brittany nodded. "Just be glad Tony and Otto aren't here."

"Where are they again?" Chloe asked as she took a seat on the bench across from us.

"They're both traveling for Thanksgiving," Brittany said. "Tony's parents moved out to Tennessee—couldn't stand the New York taxes, I guess. Or maybe it was the weather. I don't know."

"And where's Otto?" I asked.

"They go up to his uncle's cabin in the Adirondacks every year for Thanksgiving to go hunting," she said. "The hunting season is a little different up there."

I nodded, then turned to my phone. "Well, it looks like Tony found a bar anyway." I leaned over and showed the girls a picture of Tony chugging from a beer can in some dark bar.

Chloe scoffed. "Typical." She was still nursing her first drink.

Brittany shrugged. "I mean, it *is* the night before Thanksgiving. That's, like, a drinking holiday. So I guess I get it today."

Chloe and I exchanged looks. We both disagreed

with Brittany about the drinking "holiday," but kept it to ourselves.

On one of the TVs hanging over the bowling lanes they were playing the nightly news. Was it the eleven o'clock? I had lost track of time. The footage showed a local marching band, while the words: LOCAL BAND TO MARCH IN THE THANKSGIVING DAY PARADE IN NYC scrolled across the bottom.

"Oh cool! One of the high school bands is going to be in the parade tomorrow." Chloe pointed to the screen. "Ugh, I can't wait to pour myself a cup of coffee and sit on the couch in my bathrobe and watch the parade with my sisters while the food cooks."

I nodded. "I do like the parade."

"I'm usually still passed out then," Brittany muttered. "If I'm going to have to take a day off, I better do it in a haze."

"I've always wanted to see it in person," I said, ignoring Brittany's comments.

"See what in person?" Eric asked as he came back with a pitcher of beer and plastic cups.

"The Thanksgiving Day Parade," I told him. "It would make the *perfect* Thanksgiving. Especially considering my Thanksgivings usually suck."

Brittany nodded. "That would be cool. I'd love to pass out the candy to the kids."

"I'd want to be on a float and wave to the kids," Chloe said.

Eric laughed. "Yeah, and I'd like to cut the ties to the balloons and let them all go."

The girls laughed, but I interjected a fun fact I had just learned about from a video I saw in my feed. "Actually, back in the day before they cared about pollution, that's exactly what they used to do with the big balloons."

"Now *that* would be something to see." Brittany pulled a plastic cup and filled it from the pitcher.

"Those streets are probably *mobbed*," Chloe said. "Could you imagine how long people are waiting just to get a glimpse of the parade?"

"Especially when you can just watch it at home in your underwear." Eric sloppily poured himself another drink.

"I don't know," I said, trying to get the image of Eric in his underwear out of my head. "The parade route is a couple miles long. I think the crowd might not be that bad. It's not like it's New Year's Eve or anything."

"Still, those floats probably have to be registered *way* in advance," Chloe said. "I wonder if there's a waiting list to get in the parade. Or a fee—I'm sure there's a fee. There's always a fee with everything nowadays."

"Free marketing," I added. "But I'm not sure it'd be terribly hard to get on one. I see random people on those floats next to celebrities and characters all the time."

Chloe shook her head. "They're not random, Jules. They're probably a part of the team for that float—someone who works for the company but doesn't have camera time. Someone who isn't a household name. I think half the time the celebrities are the ones who are random just so they can help advertise the parade."

"Which then advertises the company." Brittany rolled her eyes. "It's all a big marketing scam, and we're falling into it."

I turned back to the TV, which had moved on to a statement about new street parking rules for the upcoming winter season.

I didn't want to believe that the parade was just a marketing gimmick. I mean, yes, of course, that was the main purpose when the parade had first started, but since then it had evolved into so much more than that. A sense of community for the whole country, which spawned millions of tiny moments of families creating traditions and memories around it over the last several decades.

"Either way," Chloe said, breaking into my thoughts. "Those people on the floats aren't just nobodies. They're real people, working hard for their companies, who deserve to be in the limelight, even if for only a few seconds a year."

"They might as well be nobodies," Eric said. "I don't know them and I don't give a shit about any of them. I don't even watch the parade. No point."

"Would you watch it if you knew someone in the parade?" I asked him.

He scoffed. "Yeah, like *that's* ever going to happen!"

The idea of Eric watching the parade at home in his underwear, as he so eloquently stated, was still stuck in my head.

"I'm just saying, I don't think it'd be that hard to get on a float," I said. "I could do it."

Brittany narrowed her eyes. She was growing skeptical of my bravado. "Okay, well, if it's not that hard then why haven't you done it?"

I averted my eyes. Where was I going with that statement anyway? It wasn't like I was ever going to get to be in the parade. Especially not when there was less than twelve hours before it started.

"Oh, I bet you could do it." Eric wrapped his arm around me and tugged me closer.

The physical touch made my heart race, but also left disappointment seeping through my veins. He gave me the awkward side-hug that he gave to everyone whenever he had had several drinks in him.

Chloe rolled her eyes. "None of you are listening to me. All of this is decided on *well* in advance! They're not just seat-fillers walking down the street in one of the biggest parades in the country!"

"In fact," Eric went on, clearly ignoring Chloe. "I *dare* you to get on a float."

Brittany broke out into a wide grin and *oohed*. "Oh man! Now you *have* to do it!" It was possible that Brittany had had too much to drink as well. "Wait, wait, wait!" She pulled out her phone and began recording me. "Julie Griffiths, do you accept the dare to get on a float in the Thanksgiving Day Parade by the end of the parade tomorrow morning?"

I froze. I couldn't turn the dare down. Not with their scrutinizing eyes on me. Not with it being recorded—which I knew would be posted immediately with my handle being tagged. Everyone online would see it as well.

"Jules, you don't have to," Chloe said from beside Brittany.

"Of course she does!" Eric blurted. "She's been *dared*."

Another moment passed, then I recovered and put on some confidence—even though it was fake. "What's my reward if I do it?"

There were several more *oohs* from around. The group of guys bowling next to us had taken interest in our conversation. Not sure how, being that Brittany and Eric were making me a spectacle and all.

Eric considered my question, then said, "I'll pay for your drinks for the rest of your life—*if* you can pull it off."

Another round of *oohs* erupted from the peanut gallery.

If Eric was my drink bitch for the rest of my life, then I would have a reason to call him up out of the blue to come and buy me a drink. I would have a reason to text him, to tease him, to spend more time with him. But I needed to make it more personal. "I need at least one meal a week in there, too."

"Greedy, huh?" Eric asked with a smirk.

I smiled back, playful. Pushing the limits of our game of cat and mouse. "Hey, a girl's gotta eat."

"Fine." Eric stuck out his hand. "*If* you can do it, you'll have one meal a week on me and drinks for life."

I smiled and shook his hand. "Then you have a deal."

Chapter Two
Thanksgiving Eve
Brian

"**B**abe, stop!" Kendra sobbed as she tugged on Brian's arm.

He ignored her and continued to shove as many of his clothes into a single duffel bag as he could fit. There were so many other things that were his throughout the apartment, but those would have to wait. Right now he just needed to get out.

"Won't you please *talk* to me?" she pleaded.

With effort, he zipped up his bag. It was nearly bursting at the seams. When he finally got it zipped closed, he slung it over his shoulder and brushed past her through the bedroom door.

"I'm sorry!" she wailed. "Brian, I'm sorry! I'm sorry I

messed everything up. If I could go back and change it all, I would!"

He stopped in the bathroom and grabbed his toothbrush and retainers—nothing about this was the clean getaway that he had been hoping for. But then, reality was usually different than TV. The truth of the matter was, without the retainers he had gotten at sixteen, the gap between his two front teeth would rear its ugly head within two days.

Salt in the wound.

His computer lay on the table beside the couch. He scooped it up and tried to find a place in his bag to shove it in. Everything was jam packed. And then there was his charger. He unplugged it from the wall, but felt resistance on the other end.

Kendra.

She looked at him with red, puffy, wet eyes, and held onto the other end of his charger. "I won't let you go until you talk to me."

He pulled on the cord, but she refused to let it go.

"Please, Brian," she said. "Stay here so we can talk this out."

Another shot against her. She had clearly forgotten that he had planned to go back home for Thanksgiving anyway. The bus ticket had been booked weeks ago. The implosion of their relationship had only removed the necessity of missing each other.

Her dark hair hung limply around her face, which was swollen and wet with tears. She really was an ugly crier. "I love you. I never wanted to hurt you."

The rage he had been shoving down erupted inside him, spilling out of his mouth.

"That's a lie!" He pointed right at her face. "You knew exactly what you were doing. So don't sit there and pretend like you didn't expect all of this to happen."

"I know! You're right! It was a mistake! I know that. But that doesn't mean we need to give up on this. On us."

"What part of my reaction came as a surprise, Kendra? Huh?" He raised his eyebrows, waiting for an answer, but none came.

"I'm sorry," she said.

"You're sorry you got caught. You *might* even be sorry that you hurt me. But you're not sorry for what you did, because you knew what you were doing all along. You made the choice, Kendra. Now you have to live with it. So all of this guilt and shame you feel, you deserve it." With another tug on the cord, it slipped from her hands.

"Okay—okay! I'm a terrible person! I did this to myself. You're right. You're right about all of it. But can't you give me a second chance? Can't we make this work?"

He wasn't sure there was any recovering from this scar in their relationship. Nor did he care to find out. He could hardly stand to look Kendra in the face for another second without seeing what she had done.

"Goodbye, Kendra," he said simply.

Without another word, he gathered his overstuffed bag, laptop, and cord, and stepped out of the apartment into the hallway, slamming the door behind him.

It wasn't until he made it down to the lobby that he found a bench nearby and opened his bag to move things around. He shoved his laptop and charging cord inside, then put his weight on it while he forced the zipper to close. It pulled at the seams, but held.

There was a train stop not far from their apartment—Kendra's apartment now. He didn't live there anymore.

He got on the train, rode it downtown to Union Station, then got in line to board a bus to New York City. A nine hour ride. One that would travel overnight, thankfully.

Toronto was the start of the bus line, so when he and the other passengers got on, they all had plenty of room in their seats. That would change with each city they stopped in along the way to the Big Apple.

Brian set his bag on the empty seat next to him,

then put up his hood and leaned against the window as it pulled away from the station.

The intent was to sleep, but his mind was spinning with having his whole world turned upside down that he knew sleep would be impossible.

He would have to move back home. Back in with his mother until he could find a place on his own. And, depending on how long it took him to extract his life from Kendra's, his mother would be his roommate for a while until he saved enough to rent his own apartment. And it wasn't like real estate in New York was cooling down anytime soon.

He would have to notify work, tell them he was coming back into the office after spending the last year working remotely. He would have to arrange another trip back to Toronto to get the rest of his stuff from the apartment. Clothes, books, several dishes, food he had helped pay for.

On second thought, he realized it was all replaceable. Anything of sentimental or significant monetary value was stuffed into the duffel bag beside him. His whole world crammed into one small little bag.

The bus slowed as the lanes in the road narrowed for the checkpoint to cross the border. Yet another step forward toward home. Toward his new life. Toward his family.

How was he going to break the news to his family? His mother adored Kendra. His brothers got along nicely with her. They had all talked about vacationing together, seeing each other for the holidays, and even doing other things together.

Thanksgiving dinner was going to be awkward.

Brian shifted in his seat as the bus lurched forward, then braked again, then lurched forward yet again. Inching forward little-by-little until the driver was finally given the approval to enter the country.

That was another thing on his to-do list: talk to immigration about ending his Canadian visa early. Brian shook his head in disappointment—embarrassment. He would have to be reminded of the things he had done to make things work with Kendra. The lengths he had gone to for that woman. All in the name of love. What a crock that turned out to be.

Not only had he moved away from his family, but he had moved to a whole different *country*—they had even discussed him applying for dual citizenship when the two of them got married.

Yeah. That definitely wouldn't be happening.

In another thirty minutes, the bus pulled up to the first stop in the United States: Buffalo.

Brian sat back and pretended he was asleep,

hoping that nobody would be willing to wake him to claim the seat beside him. Besides, it was the first stop so there were still plenty of other seats that people could take. The tactic had worked on previous trips home.

The noise level on the bus increased as people found their seats, but fifteen minutes later everyone settled. And Brian still had an empty seat beside him. At least he'd be able to get *some* sleep until the next stop in Rochester.

It was late. The overnight trips were usually not as popular as the daytime ones. Most people were more willing to sacrifice a perfectly good day in order to travel than they were to sacrifice a good night's sleep.

Brian cracked his eyes open, chancing a glance at the front. The driver was back in his seat and pulling on his seatbelt.

Home free.

Brian closed his eyes and settled back into his seat. He tried to get comfortable again, but then he heard someone talking at the front. Probably passengers trying to get comfortable and discuss seating arrangements with the strangers they needed to sit by. Brian didn't focus on what they were saying.

The bus began to pull away.

Someone nudged his shoulder. "Excuse me. Can

you please move your bag? There aren't any other seats."

His eyes flicked open and he saw a girl standing there. Probably only a few years younger than him. She had a large purse on her shoulder and she stood holding the back of the seat to steady her.

She was beautiful. Blonde hair that hung around her face, and clear blue eyes that seemed to shine, even in the nighttime dark.

But the last thing he needed at the moment was to be admiring another woman. He just wanted to be alone—to disappear from the world for a couple hours. But so far, being alone had only left him trapped by his thoughts. Maybe a passenger would help him focus on other things than letting his mind run rampant on the journey home.

"Lady, let's go! Take a seat!" the driver called from the front.

The girl turned to him with those perfect blue eyes, pleading.

Brian grumbled and sat up, pulling his heavy bag onto his lap. As the girl settled in beside him, Brian felt even more cramped in the window seat.

Between the tight confines and his running thoughts, there was certainly going to be no sleeping tonight.

Chapter Three
Thanksgiving Eve
Julie

The seats were so uncomfortable. I tried several times to readjust, finding minimal comfort on my side. The problem was, when I lay like that, I was too close to the guy sitting next to me, who was *clearly* not happy about having to share his seat.

As if it was my fault.

Finally, I got too tired of trying to get comfortable and resigned myself to the idea that I wouldn't be sleeping, like I'd hoped. Whatever alcohol I'd had at the bar had worn off. Eric, Brittany, and—begrudgingly—Chloe all chipped in for my Uber to the airport, where the Buffalo bus stop was. I had just managed to arrive by midnight, when the bus was about to pull away. Luckily,

I had the ticket information on my phone and the driver let me on.

Throughout the bus, everyone was quiet, even though it seemed that nobody could properly get to sleep. Sure, most people had their eyes closed and were *trying*, but the way each of them moved every few seconds said that their efforts were futile.

Even the guy sitting next to me was tossing and turning, trying to find a way to get comfortable sitting upright in his seat with his bag sitting in his lap.

I felt guilty for taking the empty seat next to him but it was the last one.

Well, actually, no. It wasn't the last one. There were two up near the front. One next to a guy who looked a little *too* excited at the prospect of a young college girl sitting next to him, and one next to a woman who had enough B.O. to fill the front of the bus.

That left the semi-attractive guy in the back. The one who very much did not want to share his seat. Too bad.

My phone rang, and several people turned and gave me dirty looks. I silenced it, then looked around. There were no signs that said that talking *wasn't* allowed. And it wasn't like I was going to talk as loud as I could.

So I answered.

"Hey," Chloe said on the other end. "I wanted to talk to you about that dare. I know we chipped in to Uber you to the airport, and I know you bought a ticket, but…" She took a deep breath. "Don't do it, Jules. It was just a stupid joke that Eric made. One he's probably not even going to remember in the morning. Currently, he's passed out in a booth in the bar."

It was quiet on the other end, so I assumed that Chloe stepped outside to make the call. It was kind of strange to think that they were still at the bar and I was on my way to the biggest city in the country in the middle of the night.

"Well, even if I *did* want to turn around, Chloe, your timing is terrible," I said. "I'm already on the bus. We already left."

Chloe was quiet for minute, followed only by a single, "Oh."

"Yeah," I murmured. The lady across the aisle from me continued to glare at me. As if my phone call was bothering her ability to listen to her earbuds. I was talking quietly, and the roar of the bus motor was loud enough as it was.

"Look, I'll split the bus fare with you if you want to get on a bus right away to come back," Chloe offered. "Or if you get off at the next city, I can drive out and pick you up. I've only had one, so I'd be okay to drive."

"No, Chloe, I don't want you to risk it. Besides, this is something I want to do. I bet you the first thing Eric asks when he wakes up is where the remote is so he can watch it on TV." There was more silence on the other end, so I added, "Come on, Chloe! You and I both know I dread any holiday with my family. It's not like I'm missing anything with this one. Let me make this Thanksgiving a memorable one."

Chloe sighed again. "I can't talk you out of this?"

"I don't think so."

"And you're going to be safe?"

"I promise."

"And you'll call me if you get into trouble?"

"Anytime."

"And you'll have fun?"

I cracked a smile. "That's the plan."

"Then I guess I can't stop you. Be careful, Jules."

"I will. Thanks, Chloe."

I tucked my phone back in my bag and then tried to relax. Chloe had given me an out and I stuck firm with my decision.

But was it the right one? I had never even been to New York City. Maybe Chloe was right. Maybe I should just get off in Rochester and call for a ride home.

Of course, if I called my mother, I would have to be subjected to the wrath of her and my stepdad, making Thanksgiving dinner even more unbearable than I had already expected it to be. Not to mention the endless scrutiny from my brother. And I would never be able to show my face in the bar again. Any chance at anything more with Eric would certainly be out the window. I should've suggested that he and I both come to get on the float instead of jetting off by myself and leaving him alone with Brittany.

How stupid was I?

Nope. I wasn't going to go there. I needed to change my thoughts. I *would* be successful at this. And if I wasn't? I'd have one hell of a story to tell.

The guy beside me shifted in his seat again. He clearly was not catching any Zs. When he turned and saw me looking at him, he scrunched his eyebrows together as if to say, "What are you looking at?"

Instead, I smiled and offered my hand. "Hi, I'm Julie."

He glared at me, but sat up straighter, adjusting the bag in his lap, then pulled his hood off and shook my hand. "I'm Brian." He turned back to the window, not engaging in anymore conversation.

"Where are you headed to?" I asked.

"New York," he murmured, eyes still trained out the window. We couldn't see much in the darkness.

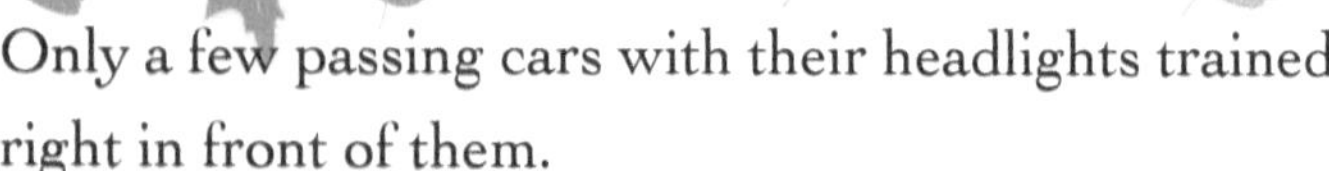

Only a few passing cars with their headlights trained right in front of them.

"Oh wow! That's where I'm going too! Are you going for the parade?"

Another glare in my direction, then, "No, I'm going home for Thanksgiving."

My eyes widened. "You *live* in New York City?" My voice was louder than I expected and several people around us cleared their throats, which had nothing to do with the chillier temperatures springing up illnesses.

Of course I knew that New York City had a population of over eight million people, but I hadn't really met anyone my own age from there. Sure, I had met people from *down state* in college, but they seemed to be from the outskirts of "the city."

Or maybe it was that they told me the names of places within the city and I just didn't know where those places were. Until Eric had challenged me, I had had no real interest in going to New York City. So much had changed in such little time.

"Uh…yeah, I guess that's where I live now." He seemed to sober as he considered my question. With his hood off, I could see that he was more than just *semi*-attractive. Still, his attitude was off-putting.

"You guess?" I asked. "Are you, like, moving or something?"

Another pause as he considered. "Yeah, I guess I am." He turned his body back toward the window, quietly telling me that he didn't want to talk.

That never bothered me. I laughed a little to myself. "You guess a lot."

He shrugged.

I fiddled with the strap on my bag. "Well, I'm going to New York City on a dare to see if I can get on a float in the parade."

Brian looked over at me. "You mean the big televised one?"

"Mm-hmm," I said with a nod.

"You're crazy."

Now it was my turn to shrug. As he continued to look at me with wild eyes, I laughed again. "I know I'm crazy. And that this idea is a little wild—"

"A *little* wild?"

"What's the worst that can happen?"

"The worst that can happen is that you get arrested."

My lips formed into a giant *O* as the realization hit me. *Of course* there would security and police patrolling throughout the parade. Any violators, no matter how innocent, would have to face legal repercussions. Was I making a mistake? I supposed it was too late to back down now.

Brian sighed and sat up. "Here's what you need to do: find a float that has costumed characters — but only the ones who stand and wave. You don't want the ones who have to dance or anything. Then, if you can convince one of them to let you wear their costume instead of them, you can sneak on the float undetected."

"You think it's that easy?"

"I wouldn't say it's *easy*, but I think that's your best bet. Those people in the costumes probably go to the parade every year. All they want is the paycheck. As long as you're not taking that from them, then sure, I think you could swing it."

I smirked, glad that I hooked him into a conversation so I didn't have to sit alone. "The trouble is, in order for me to win the dare, my friends need to be able to see me on camera. If I put on a character costume, they won't be able to see me unless I take the costume off — and scar millions of children watching in the process."

Brian laughed at that. "Who even proposed this dare?"

Now it was my turn to look away. "Just a friend of mine."

"Well, it sounds like they were setting you up to fail by creating all of these rules."

"He didn't set *rules*," I blurted. "But it makes

sense that he needs to be able to see me in order to know I was there."

"He can't just take your word for it?"

My shoulders began to raise up. "Well…I don't know…"

"Sounds to me like you could've snapped a few pictures and sent them as proof enough. Your friend doesn't trust that you won't cheat?"

"Okay, *stranger*, you don't need to be critiquing my life—and my *friends*, who you don't even know!"

"Fine, I won't critique your friends, but I'll critique their stupid idea. It's stupid."

I raised my eyebrows. "Wow. What a great comeback."

"I'm not really sure how to dumb it down anymore."

I rolled my eyes. Now I was regretting striking up a conversation with this arrogant jerk. "Never mind." I turned away from him and focused on the man who was sleeping three rows up. It looked like he was about to fall out of his seat and into the aisle. I wondered how many bumps in the road or sudden turns it would take to get him to topple over.

"Look," Brian said from beside me. "I'm sorry for saying this idea is stupid—don't get me wrong, I still think that. I'm just sorry for saying it out loud."

"Is this supposed to be an apology?"

"Of sorts. If you're really dead-set on doing this, I guess I can help you figure out how."

"Really?" I was suddenly more excited than I expected. The burden of having to figure it all out on my own had been weighing on me and I didn't even realize it until someone offered relief. I didn't know the city. I didn't know how the parade was planned. I didn't know how I was going to pull this off. I didn't really know anything.

He nodded. "Yep. You need a new plan."

"That's it? That's your big advice?"

"Can you blame me? I've never even thought of doing something so stupid before. And you've given me — what? — five minutes to figure this out for you?"

I rolled my eyes again and turned back to the man about to topple over. His neck was jarred in such an uncomfortable position that I wondered briefly if he might be dead. But then he snorted and shifted a little, proving that life was still present. A Thanksgiving miracle.

"Let me think about this," Brian muttered from beside me. "Maybe you can hang around the parade starting point to look for an opening."

I looked over at him. "The parade starting point?"

"Well, yeah. It has to start somewhere, right?"

"I guess I never really thought about it. But sure,

that sounds about right."

He narrowed his eyes. "You haven't put any thought into this at all, have you?"

"I've known about this for—" I checked the time on my phone. "—only about three hours!"

"You were only dared three hours ago and now you're on a bus across the state? That's a little…impulsive."

I shrugged. "Sometimes you have to be impulsive. That's where the best stories come from, right?"

He didn't say anything, but the expression on his face said enough. He was judging me. Hardcore.

Then again, even I could agree that this plan, in hindsight, *was* kind of stupid. But my pride wouldn't let me admit that out loud.

"Yes, there's a parade starting point," Brian went on. "If you head up there, they're probably using some of the park to—"

"Central Park," I cut in, boasting my little knowledge of New York City.

"Yes…" he said slowly, then added, "Do you have any idea where the parade route starts?"

"Central Park," I said with a proud smile.

"You do realize that Central Park stretches, like, fifty blocks, right? It's huge."

"And?"

"And you can't just say it starts at the park, you

need to know *where* in the park."

"Do *you* know where?" I pressed. Mr. Smarty-Pants was flaunting his knowledge now. I wasn't a dumb girl. Okay, sure, maybe this trip wasn't my most shining example of a *good* idea, but I was certainly smarter than it seemed.

"Central Park West and 78th Street," he said. "Near the museum."

"And you just *happened* to know that?"

He looked a little defensive. "I was reading an article about it the other day and I thought it was interesting."

A man who read. Who had ever heard of that?

"Do you have any idea where that is?" he asked.

"The park!" I said with a laugh.

He closed his eyes, took a deep breath, and gently nodded. "Yes. By the park. Have you even been to New York before?"

"I live in New York," I said.

"I meant New York *City*."

"Oh! No."

He shook his head. "You're going to need more help than just coming up with a plan."

I smiled. "You seem like you know your way around town, being that you're a New Yorker and all. Why don't you help me?" As I said the words, I wondered if I would regret them. Then again, it wasn't as if I hadn't been around arrogance before. My defense mechanism to that was to deflect to humor.

"I don't…" he started, but then stopped when my face began to droop with disappointment. It hadn't been my intent to guilt him into it, but I couldn't help the look on my face as all my wildest dreams came crashing down with his denial.

We were quiet as the proposal, and the beginning of a rejection, hung in the air between us.

Finally, he said, "Okay. I'll help you. But you need to trust my advice."

"Done."

"And you need to listen."

"We'll see."

"And if the police start poking around, I'm out."

"Understandable." I smiled again and offered my hand for the second time. "So…do we have a deal?"

He let out a heavy breath of air, then took my hand. "Fine. Deal."

It was the second deal I made that night. But I felt good about this one.

THANK YOU

Thank you to the DN Publishing VIP Club members over at Patreon! Become a member and enjoy weekly perks!

Tracy O'Neil

Marguerite Goosby

Kanyon Kiernan

patreon.com/DNPublishing

ACKNOWLEDGMENTS

This project would not have been possible without the support of my Kickstarter backers! Thank you all for your support!

Heiko Koenig

Anonymous Reader

Julie McAtee

Marguerite Goosby

Christy S

John Idlor

Kanyon N.

Florentina

Michele R

Michele

Lanah De Witt

Jessie moved back to picturesque Montana Beach after a heartbreaking split with her ex. She's since thrown herself into her grandparent's inn, which has been struggling financially thanks to the town having seen better days. With few options available, Jessie considers accepting a developer's offer to buy Montana Manor, seeing it as a way to save her family's legacy, until she learns that he wants to tear it down.

Meanwhile, Mason's tired of working at his father's advertising firm in New York City, although his father wants him to become his replacement. Unsure if that's the course he wants his life to take, Mason escapes to Montana Beach and the only inn in town to consider the proposal. But after he meets Jessie, he seems to gain only another reason not to take up his father's offer.

When Mason offers to help Jessie launch a campaign to save Montana Manor, the two quickly find themselves relying more and more on each other. But summer doesn't last forever, and Mason's stay is coming to an end.

Summer Stay is the first book in the Montana Beach series. Available in hardcover, paperback, ebook, and audiobook!

www.DavidNethBooks.com/MontanaBeach

Autumn Chapman is the fourth-generation owner of her family's struggling apple orchard. Her uncles, who are co-owners, want to sell what's left and walk away while they still can, but Autumn doesn't want to let the legacy of her family's business die with her. However, the finances are tight and sales are slowing year-to-year.

Braden Clinton is a young executive at a large suburban conglomerate. With the promise of a promotion, he's been tasked with getting the Chapmans to sell their business to further expand his company's portfolio. The problem? Autumn refuses to sell.

Not willing to take no for an answer, Braden decides to show up to the orchard every day to convince Autumn to sell. But as he learns more and more about the orchard, Autumn, and her family's business, he starts to think that maybe he is on the wrong side of the fight. Meanwhile Autumn starts to think that maybe she can't keep the business afloat on her own.

www.DavidNethBooks.com/d-allen-standalones

More by the Author

To find more books by the author, visit
DavidNethBooks.com/Books

* * *

Subscribe to his newsletter to be the first to know of new releases and special deals!
DavidNethBooks.com/Newsletter

* * *

If you enjoyed the book, please consider leaving a review on Goodreads or the retailer you bought it from. Reviews help potential readers determine whether they'll enjoy a book, so any comments on what you thought of the story would be very helpful!

About the Author

D. Allen is the author of the sweet small town romance series, Montana Beach and Small Town Christmas.

Also writes fantasy and superhero fiction as David Neth.

www.DavidNethBooks.com
www.facebook.com/DavidNethBooks
www.instagram.com/dnpublishing
www.patreon.com/DNPublishing

9 781963 602777